By ANDREW GREY

Published by DREAMSPINNER PRESS
www.dreamspinnerpress.com

Published by DREAMSPINNER PRESS
www.dreamspinnerpress.com

Published by DREAMSPINNER PRESS
www.dreamspinnerpress.com

FIRE AND OBSIDIAN
ANDREW GREY

Published by
DREAMSPINNER PRESS

5032 Capital Circle SW, Suite 2, PMB# 279,
Tallahassee, FL 32305-7886 USA
www.dreamspinnerpress.com

Fire and Obsidian
© 2019 Andrew Grey.

Cover Art
© 2019 Kanaxa.

Mass Market Paperback ISBN: 978-1-64108-491-8
Trade Paperback ISBN: 978-1-64405-378-2
Digital ISBN: 978-1-64405-377-5
Library of Congress Control Number: 2018914534
Mass Market Paperback published June 2023
v. 1.0

Printed in the United States of America
∞
This paper meets the requirements of
ANSI/NISO Z39.48-1992 (Permanence of Paper).

To police officers everywhere who work to protect each and every one of us.

CHAPTER 1

"THERE IS no such thing as a victimless crime," Mattias Dumont said as he slowly walked up the rows of tables filled with men and women in uniform. "And I hate thieves. They're selfish and care very little for others. They steal other people's hopes and dreams, their livelihoods. They're part of the reason all of us pay so much for insurance… because there is a victim for every crime. It's you, me, and everyone else. I really do hate theft, so it sucks that I'm so good at it."

He'd held the gaze of every person in the room up until that point. Then the deputies began looking at one another, some maybe even wondering if this was a test and they should take action.

A hand finally went up.

"Yes?"

"You're bullshitting us," the officer said. "You have to be."

Mattias came to a stop at the front of the room and leaned back slightly against the table. "The statute of limitations on all my crimes expired a few years ago, and if you look me up, you'll find next to nothing." Okay, now he was bragging a little, but that was the fun part for him.

"Because you did nothing," someone whispered from the back.

Mattias lifted his gaze from the front of the room to the back where a tall, broad-chested, jet-black-haired beauty stood, his arms folded over his suited chest. No uniform for this man. He was someone special. Mattias ignored the way his heart beat a little faster, the same way it had when he first touched an object he'd planned and studied for months to acquire. He'd always told himself he'd been in the acquisition business—he acquired things from their owners without their permission, often without their knowledge… sometimes for months.

Mattias kept his eye on Mr. Perfectly Pressed Suit as he continued his talk. "You won't find anything on me because I didn't get caught. Being a good thief isn't like in the movies. There's no *Ocean's Eleven*… or some such crap where you try to see who can pull off the biggest or the best heist. A cache of small gems that can easily be removed from their settings and would be hard to trace is perfection. I made a very good living under the radar. I didn't take the Hope Diamond, but I did steal from many people." To him it had been a profession, one that had gone sour over time.

"Prove it," Mr. Perfectly Pressed Suit said from the back.

The others in the room puffed out their chests, their police officer confidence kicking in.

"All right. Everyone stand up, please," Mattias said calmly. "Someone identify an object that you want me to take."

One of the officers held up a watch. It was plain and nothing that would ever have interested him during his career, but for demonstration purposes, it would do.

"Perfect. Put that back on, and I'll demonstrate. I'd like you all to stay standing as I attempt to take the watch." Mattias cleared his throat and pretended to think about how he was going to proceed. He wandered up and down each aisle, working his way over to the officer in question, who stood near the back, in the far aisle, with another officer in front and in back of him.

Mattias kept his expression neutral, as though he were concentrating, his gaze rarely wavering from his quarry. As he got closer, he nodded to the officer, whose gaze locked on to him. Mattias could almost feel his quarry's heart rate increase the closer he got. This man knew something was going to happen, and he was prepared for it. Mattias turned the corner, anticipation building in the room, so thick that he could taste it. Every eye was on either him or his quarry, which was fine. Mattias was calm and cool, no worries. As he got closer, his quarry's arm jittered slightly. Mattias watched it for a second and then lifted his head, meeting the gaze of the men and women around him. Passing by his quarry, Mattias smiled and continued back up to the front of the room.

"I still have the watch," the officer said, holding up his wrist, and the others in the room clapped.

"I guess you aren't as good as you thought."

Mattias waited until the ruckus and self-congratulations died down and they all turned back to him. He cleared his throat. "And you are?" It was best to confront this type of adversary head-on.

"Detective James Levinson. I'm working with the sheriff's department as a consultant on the robberies in the area." His steely gaze held Mattias's, and he didn't

look away. It was a test of wills, and Mattias enjoyed it,
especially from the stunning man who made his body
temperature rise and his heart beat a little faster just
from the intensity in his eyes. This was a man who
didn't back down from a fight and who held tightly to
his convictions. Mattias's lips curled upward. He got
the feeling that this was also a man who never admitted
he was wrong. Good. Mattias liked that.

Mattias was going to love making him eat his
words.

"Let's see. Being a good thief is about doing what
isn't expected." He reached into his pocket, pulled out
a wallet, and opened it. "Pierre Ravelle." He smiled and
held up the wallet. "I believe this is yours." The others
in the room snickered as Pierre approached and accepted his wallet back. "No hard feelings," Mattias said as
he handed it over.

Pierre blushed slightly and returned to his seat.
"Come on, guys," Pierre said, to try to stop their
razzing.

"Pierre isn't alone." Mattias began emptying the
inner pockets of his jacket of their contents, including
one more wallet, a pair of handcuffs, and a flashlight,
as well as half a dozen other things. "Check to see what
you're missing and come up to retrieve it in a moment,"
Mattias said, then slowly reached into an inner pocket,
close to his body. He used his fingertips to pull out the
service revolver and gently lay it on the table.

The room went silent, with each officer checking
his belt.

"Detective Levinson, I believe this belongs to
you." He kept the smile off his face, watching as the
detective checked inside his coat and then stormed up,

grabbed his revolver, checked it, and slipped it back into its holster.

"Now there are hard feelings," the detective whispered in a growl that under different circumstances would be sexy as all hell. Mattias swallowed hard and tried to put that voice and the way it sent a jolt of electricity running through him out of his mind.

"As I was saying," Mattias began after Detective Levinson had returned to his position, and the others had retrieved their lifted articles, "thieves rarely do what is expected." He once again leaned against the table in a relaxed stance. "I have done this same demonstration a number of times, and it's always the same. You're all trained and highly skilled police officers, so naturally you don't think you can be the victim of a crime, but anyone and everyone is vulnerable." He crossed his arms over his chest.

"How does this help us with this rash of robberies in the county?"

"Excellent question"—Mattias moved forward to see his name tag—"Deputy Brown. I will be working with each of you to try to learn how these thieves are operating, and then I will try to get into their heads to figure out where they might strike and how we as a department can get one step ahead of them."

"This little demonstration....," Detective Levinson said, clearly still smarting from Mattias's applied skill.

"It was to earn your trust and to prove to all of you that I am good at what I do and that I can help you. For the record, I am a thief, or I was, just like I told you. Now I run my own consulting company, and I work with law enforcement to catch and apprehend people like the man I used to be." Mattias held the edge of the table. "Do you have any questions?" A bunch of hands shot into the air. Mattias pointed to the man whose wallet he had taken.

"Deputy Pierre Ravelle," he said, identifying himself, then cleared his throat. "Will you be working directly with those of us on patrol?"

"I haven't been assigned to anyone specific yet. But the best thing you can do is keep your eyes open. Our thieves will be doing a number of things. They will be looking for victims and relatively easy, portable items."

Ravelle's hand went up again. "I work mostly in the courthouse...."

Mattias nodded. "You do realize that's a great place to case people. There are plenty of lawyers, and some of them represent well-to-do clients. They wear expensive watches, and clients may have jewelry and other items. It surprises me the number of people who actually overdress for court. Keep an eye out for people who shouldn't be there. I once cased a potential mark by posing as a garbage man. I hauled away their trash for a week. I learned plenty about them, and no one was the wiser. They had a security force, but they never looked twice at me." He raised his eyebrows as deputies nodded. "There are a million ways to hide in plain sight. Part of what we're going to do today is learn how to do some of that so you can learn the signs to look out for."

"What kind of signs?" a deputy asked.

"Not the ones you see on TV. There aren't going to be men hiding in TV repair vans or things like that. But a good way to be unobtrusive is as a painter. They wear coveralls, great for hiding tools and small pieces of equipment. They're covered in splotches, so people don't want to get too close in case they get paint on them. They're left alone and can often wander through a building or crowd unobstructed. If I were casing the courthouse and wanted to be unobtrusive, I'd dress as a lawyer."

"But everyone has to go through security," Deputy Ravelle said.

"Yes, they do. Remember that the building is public, though. You can restrict what people bring in, but not who can enter. Everyone has a right to access the government services inside the building, and if they're dressed as a lawyer, who is going to give them a second thought regarding wherever they go in the building? Like I said, it isn't likely someone is going to be robbed in the courthouse, but it's a great place for people watching. So while they may be watching you, it's important that you are on the lookout for them."

With his introduction complete, Mattias started in on the meat of his presentation to give the deputies some things to watch out for. The session was scheduled to last all morning, and Mattias could readily admit that they were a good group. They listened, asked questions, and really seemed to want to know what could be done to stop what was happening. Of course, Mattias was keenly aware of the hard and continuous stare of Detective Levinson. He had given this type of presentation dozens of times and worked with a number of police organizations all over the country, but he'd never been as self-conscious as he was under the detective's gaze. Something about him got under Mattias's skin, and he had no idea what it was.

"Thank you all for your attention. I hope I get the chance to work with as many of you as possible," Mattias said at the end of his presentation.

The deputies stood, and many of them came forward to shake his hand, including Deputy Ravelle, which Mattias took as a good sign.

"That went well," he told himself as he gathered his things to leave the room.

"I don't know about that," Levinson said as he stalked up toward Mattias. "You could have gotten yourself shot in a room full of cops if anyone had caught you. How would that have gone over?"

"Detective Levinson, I can lift the gun out of a policeman's holster on a routine traffic stop if I want to, and there's little he can do about it." Mattias sat on the edge of the front table. "I have to give a demonstration in order for them to understand my capabilities, which I only gave them a glimpse of, and for them to understand how easy it is for thieves to get what they want, especially professional ones. And that's what you're dealing with, I'm pretty sure." He smiled. "Think of it as an attention-getter."

Detective Levinson rolled his eyes. "I think of it as a fox in the henhouse." He crossed his arms over his chest. "And don't think I won't be keeping an eye on you. I don't care what fancy title you give yourself or who hires you now. You're still a thief."

"Probably." Mattias leaned forward and waited until curiosity got the better of the detective and he lowered his arms. The he pressed something small and metal into Levinson's hand. "Maybe I can't help myself." He looked deeply into Levinson's dark brown eyes, which bordered on fathomless. "Maybe it's a compulsion. You know what that is, don't you?" He parted his lips, and damn it all to heaven if Levinson's eyes didn't widen and his breathing pick up a little at his taunt. For a second his upper lip quivered, desire flashing across his features, but it was quickly schooled away. Not that it mattered to Mattias—a second of true insight was worth more than hours of boring recon.

"That's…." Levinson paused as he raised his hand upward, scowling at the Swiss Army knife that rested there. "You better keep your son-of-a-bitch hands out of my pockets or so help me—"

A brisk knock on the door interrupted his tirade, and Mattias stepped back.

The door opened, and one of the deputies from the back of the class poked his head inside. "Sheriff Briggs wants to see both of you right now," he said.

Detective Levinson dropped his knife back into his pocket and straightened his suit. He turned toward the door and stopped. "You go first, where I can keep an eye on you," he growled.

Mattias chuckled softly, pulling the door open the rest of the way and leaving the room. There was something perversely rewarding about putting an otherwise-confident man just a little ill at ease. Hell, it could be downright fun, and as one of his foster mothers had told him years before, it was one of his supreme talents.

Mattias followed the deputy through the station and to the closed sheriff's office door. He knocked and received a call to come inside. "Good afternoon, Sheriff Briggs," Mattias said as he entered the office and sat in the far chair across the desk from him. "I believe congratulations are in order for your appointment." He reached out to shake his hand.

"Thanks. I'm still only temporarily appointed until the next election in November." Sheriff Briggs waited until Levinson came in, and had him close the door. "But that isn't going to happen unless we break up this ring of thieves that has been operating in the county. They've struck from Mechanicsburg to Carlisle to Camp Hill. Even the rural areas have been hit, which is why it's ended up on our plate. The various city departments have jurisdiction in their areas, but since this is bigger than any of them, they have all backed away and given us the go-ahead to take the entire case across the municipalities." He leaned forward, his hard gaze landing on both of them. "I brought you both in to work on this, find out what's going on, and bring them all in. Detective, you are the lead, and I'll have two of my best men working with you. Dumont, you are a consultant assigned to Levinson and the team. You have a reputation for understanding criminals like the ones we're after."

"Yes," Mattias agreed softly, reaching for the file as the sheriff handed it over. Detective Levinson took it out of the sheriff's hand before he could, and Mattias stifled a groan. So this was how things were going to be, a pissing match? Well, he was more than up for it.

"Ravelle and Brown will be assigned to your team. They are both good deputies with a lot of experience, and they know their jobs and the county very well. If you need anything, you're to let me know, and I will allocate the necessary resources. This entire situation has much of the public on edge. The news media is calling it a crime spree, and every night there's some new story that is freaking people out. Homes have been entered during the day while people are home. They get in and out without being heard or seen, except by a few neighbors. The names of the people who might have seen them are in the file. Talk to them again, get whatever you can, and put these people out of business. And do it fast." His eyes blazed, and Mattias nodded.

"I'm sure the detective and I will work as quickly as we can." There was nothing else for him to add. Mattias had only seen the barest details up to this point. What he needed was a look at that file, and Levinson was holding it as though it were the Holy Grail.

"James," Briggs said as he turned to Levinson, "you need to work as a team. You've gotten good results much of the time, but you won't be able to solve this puzzle without teamwork and some help." He stood. "I brought both of you in because you are the best at what you do. Now I expect you to work together." He leaned forward. "And you will." There was no arguing with that tone.

Mattias had never worked with Sheriff Briggs before, but then, he often worked with new chiefs and departments. What was clear was that Sheriff Briggs and the detective had a history.

"I understand," James said, and the sheriff turned to Mattias. It was surprising how easily Mattias's brain glommed on to the detective's first name and held on to it.

"He's a good cop, but he tends to do things on his own, and that isn't what's needed here." Sheriff Briggs turned back to James. "Work together and get these people. There is way too much that's disappearing."

Mattias cleared his throat. "If I can ask, how long have you two known each other?" It was best if he knew what sort of political environment he was walking into.

"James and I went to the academy together in Philadelphia," Sheriff Briggs explained. "We were roommates for a while as well. Even then James was a superstar." He turned to James, and his expression softened. "You lived and breathed police work, always have. But

I've come to realize that one of the keys to solving cases and getting convictions is teamwork." His expression grew pointed, and Mattias wondered what was behind the comment. He didn't dare ask, and filed it away for later. "I'd love to have you on my team here, but I can't do that if you won't work with them. We are too small a department for renegades." He drummed his fingers on the desk, and James and Mattias stood. Clearly they had received their orders and were being dismissed.

"You deserve this position, Solly, and I'll do everything I can to make sure you get elected," James said.

Mattias headed for the door, feeling a bit like an intruder on a private conversation. He opened the office door, stepped out, and closed it again. If they wanted to talk privately, that was their business.

"Mathias," one of the officers said, getting his attention.

"Mattias," he corrected as he stopped.

"Sorry. I'm Clay Brown, and you know Pierre. We've been assigned to the robbery team." Both men shook his hand, and Pierre patted him on the shoulder.

"No hard feelings, though maybe you could show me how you got my wallet so easily." He smiled and turned to Clay, who nodded. "The more we know about thieves and thieving, the more we can help people."

"Of course. I'll be happy to show you anything I can." They seemed like good enough guys. "Where are we working?"

"I got us a small room off the squad area. That way we can gather our information and keep it in one place. I got some boards and stuff so we can share ideas." They were both clearly excited to be working on this.

"This sort of thing can be tough to crack."

"We aren't afraid of hard work."

"Pierre and I are looking to advance, and we think this is a good way to do it." They opened the door and followed Mattias inside. The room itself was sparse, with serviceable furniture, a table that was scarred from years of use, and, as promised, whiteboards and a corkboard. "Where do we start?"

"James has the files, so we'll need to wait for him and then have a look, unless you guys know something?" Mattias asked, and they shrugged.

"No details, just rumors so far."

Clay snickered. "I have this theory that it's surfers who came in here to ride the waves on the creek off Children's Lake in Boiling Springs." He snickered, and Pierre rolled his eyes.

"Nice *Point Break* reference. You a Gary Bussey fan?"

They both shook their heads. "Keanu Reeves," they answered in unison, then laughed.

Well, that told him something interesting… very interesting. "He was hot then, wasn't he?"

The door opened and James strolled in, closing the door before dropping the file on the table with a paper smack. Pierre took it, and Mattias waited for James to say something. "What was hot?" James asked, slipping off his suit jacket.

"Well, actually, we were just musing on how hot a certain detective was in his suit and tie." Dang, it was fun to see James put off his game. "But now that you're here, we should get down to work." Mattias pulled out a chair and sat. "Let's go over the crimes, how they got in, what they took, time of day—all of that."

"It's in there," James sniped. "You can read as well as the rest of us."

"And we can either get to work or have a pissing contest," Mattias said. "Let's get to work. Lay out as much detail as we can and see if there are any patterns. If this is a small group of people, then there will be patterns of some sort. Thieves stick to what works—get the goods and move on. They don't reinvent the wheel for each heist. Like I said, this isn't an *Ocean's* movie." Mattias sat back, watching James as he pulled out the chair at the far end of the table, plopped into it, and reached for the file.

"Ravelle, would you do the honors?" James asked, handing him a red dry-erase marker.

Mattias lifted his messenger bag onto the table and pulled out a small laptop. He opened it and started entering the information into a spreadsheet as they wrote it on the board.

"What are you doing?" James asked.

"Going high-tech. If it's in here, we can search and rearrange it much more easily. I'm also hoping to see if the MO matches anyone I know." Mattias raised his eyebrows. "No loyalty among thieves and all that." He cocked what he hoped was a wicked grin and got back to work, listing the details as James and Clay called them out, going through nearly a dozen higher-end robberies.

CHAPTER 2

ONCE A thief, always a thief. That was how James felt. He had seen too many people ride the revolving door of the justice system, and all too rarely did they ever change. There had been more people caught and prosecuted for the same crime over and over than he could possibly count. And it galled him to take suggestions from a self-professed lawbreaker, especially one who had in effect disarmed him. But he didn't have any choice. If he wanted reassignment and this case solved so his old friend could be elected as sheriff, a position he more than deserved, then he needed to put up with the man. That didn't mean he was going to trust him any farther than he could throw him.

"Have you come up with anything?" James asked once they had been through all the case files.

Mattias chuckled. "Did you really expect me to be able to take a single look at this and have all the answers for you?" He smiled. "I'm good, but not quite that good." He returned to looking at his damned spreadsheet. "There are some things that stand out only because they're pretty expected. A lot of the thefts are jewelry, and not superexpensive items either. They would be easy to fence or liquidate." He turned to

James. "I suggest you check auction records to try to match up some of the items. These are just the kind of things that could be consigned to an auction house and easily sold."

James stifled a growl. "We've already done that with the items from Mechanicsburg before turning over the cases, with no luck. If they are being auctioned, it's outside the area." That meant it was nearly impossible to trace.

Mattias pulled out one particular case file and handed it to him. "Check out that one, please. The third item down on the list."

James took the sheet. "Okay. It's a locket inscribed 'From Victoria.'"

Mattias rolled his eyes. "No. That's someone's sloppy notes. I've seen one of those lockets. Look at the description more closely—it's inlaid with a few pearls and a picture of Victoria. That's *Queen* Victoria. She had a number of those lockets made and gave them out as tokens during her reign. There can't be that many here in the US, so we may be able to trace this item if the thieves are stupid enough to try to sell it here."

James peered at the report. "Sounds like something quite valuable."

"Three or four thousand dollars is my guess, more in the UK." Mattias glanced up at him. "But this is specific. If I had stolen something like this, I'd either hold it for a period of time or simply carry it with me and sell it on another end of the country or overseas. Moving items, particularly small things, is quite easy. Still, one of the ways we might catch them is if they make a mistake." He took back the page and put it in the case file where it had been. "Maybe we should contact the victims again and see if there is anything else that's gotten misdocumented."

James wanted to argue, but Mattias was probably right. "Pierre, you and Clay split the list and talk to the victims again. Tell them that we're trying to make some progress and it would really help if they could tell us if there was anything particularly special about the items taken. I'm going to see if I can contact the potential eyewitnesses for anything else they might be able to give us." James took down the names, addresses, and phone numbers, sitting at the table to make calls and see if he could catch any of them at home. Two of them were, and he left messages with the others before grabbing his coat and heading for the door.

"What about me?" Mattias asked as he stood.

"I can do this alone." In fact, James preferred that.

"Yeah, you probably can, but I'm not going to sit here and wait around for all of you." Mattias closed his computer, slipped it into his bag, and slung the strap over his shoulder, turning to him expectantly. "Briggs said we were to work together, and I don't think that means you going off on your own like this."

Damn it all, there was a slight curl at the corner of his lips.

"Fine. But you stay out of the way and don't say anything. You can listen." James headed for the door, then strode as fast as he could out to his car. Mattias was already in the passenger seat before he got in, the bag on his lap. James buckled himself in and pulled out of the lot, heading back toward his home turf. Neither of them talked, and after a while, it put James on edge, which he didn't like. "What are you thinking?"

"That I shouldn't talk."

James wanted to strangle him. "Are you always this annoying?" he asked as he pulled to a stop at a light on their way east.

"Maybe just a little more than usual. You tend to bring it out in me." Mattias smiled and his eyes glistened. For a second it was like Mattias had been transformed into some ancient god. Maybe he was the reborn spirit of the mischievous god of wine or something. "I'm sorry I lifted your gun. I didn't know you were going to take it that harshly, but you were so stoic and uptight."

"I'm professional. I have a job to do, and I do it the very best I can. All the time." There hadn't been much room for anything or anyone else in his life. He was the job—he lived the job.

"I see," Mattias said as he turned to him. For a second James felt naked, as though Mattias could see straight through him. He wanted to squirm but wasn't going to show Mattias the weakness.

"What does that mean?" James snapped, then immediately wished he hadn't.

"Look, I'm sorry, okay? I didn't mean to take anything away from your professionalism when I lifted your gun. You challenged me, and I think I tried to get back at you a little. Believe it or not, I'm just as much a professional as you are." Mattias hit him with a stare.

It was on the tip of his tongue to make a crack about Mattias's "profession," but James figured letting it go was probably going to be more productive. They needed to work together on this case, and fighting with each other wasn't going to get the job done.

"I saw that glare." There was teasing around the edges of Mattias's voice, and James figured he was trying to ramp him up again. "I am a professional—I always have been. I never injured anyone or damaged things of value. I was a thief, yes. I got in and out quick and easy, and that was the end of it."

James cleared his throat. "How does one go about getting into that 'profession'? Did you go to thief college? Get a bachelors in burglary?" He was trying to be funny, but it didn't sound like that.

"No. I grew up in group and foster homes and learned what I know from the other kids... at least to start. You know, the ones who had been in jail or spent time in juvy. They're great places to learn about stealing jewelry, picking pockets, and boosting cars." Mattias crossed his arms over his chest again. "Not everything is the perfect life that you had. Let me guess—two parents, two point five kids, two cars.... I get the drift. Well, I had none, and I was good, so I figured out a way to survive." Mattias turned away, looking out the window.

Damn, that so wasn't the kind of thing that James had been expecting to hear. He swallowed hard and concentrated on his driving. His own insecurities bubbled too close to the surface. James took a deep breath and pushed his thoughts back to where they belonged. He was on the job, and that was a lot easier to think about and concentrate on than his own miserable upbringing. Yeah, it sounded like Mattias didn't have a picnic childhood, but the notion that James had had it easy was off the mark as well. Still, Mattias could think whatever he wanted to; it didn't matter in the least. They were here to do a job, and James intended to see that through, nothing more. The fact that Mattias smelled like a spring morning was nothing, just like the way he bit his lower lip, worrying it between his teeth, didn't matter either. Nor did the intensity in his eyes, tinged with vulnerability, that made James wonder what he'd been through. He shook his head slightly. James wasn't going there.

He cleared his throat, needing to get the conversation back where it belonged. "The people we're going to see have already met with the police once, so we need to be polite and understanding of their feelings."

"Are they victims themselves?" Mattias asked.

"No. But seeing a crime can have an effect on people. They feel for their neighbors and want to help. So sometimes they add things. It isn't malicious, but either they want to make us happy or their mind is filling in details for them. It happens. Just let me ask the questions, and we'll see if we can get anything more helpful than in the original interview." James tried to calm himself, gripping the wheel tighter, attempting to channel his discomfort into something useful. He kept his eyes on the road, even as he felt Mattias's gaze on him.

The thing was, under normal circumstances he'd be a little creeped out, but having Mattias watch him was different. He turned up the air-conditioning a little to try to head off the rising heat under his collar. Why did it have to be a guy like Mattias who got under his skin this way? He had left behind the things that Mattias represented, turned his back on that, and he needed to get it together. *Be professional* echoed through his mind. That was the way for him to get through this. It was only until they found out what was going on, and then James could walk away and go back to his ordered life without this flip-flopping in his belly. And if he were honest, without wondering about what was under those stylish clothes of Mattias's.

"I'll let you take the lead," Mattias said.

James wondered why he didn't completely believe it. Not that he had time to talk it over further as they pulled into the driveway of their first witness. He turned off the engine, and they got out and headed to the front door, which opened to a woman with a baby on her hip and a little girl of about four with dark brown pigtails.

He introduced himself, and Mattias as a consultant working with their department. It was a nice afternoon, and they sat in the wicker furniture on the porch, the little girl sitting next to her mama. "I know you already spoke to the police, but we were hoping you might have remembered something else."

"I only saw them for a few seconds. I was home taking care of the kids. A white work van—you know, the kind plumbers and stuff use—pulled up, and I didn't think anything of it. The Nelsons have been doing some renovations. I didn't put the pieces together until I heard they had been robbed, and then I asked if they had had some workman there." She put the baby on her shoulder and patted his back to calm his fussiness. "I really didn't see the men or anything else."

The little girl slipped off the chair and onto the porch floor, then slid under the chair and pulled a doll out from under it. She jumped up and down a few times and then settled near Mattias to play.

"Is that your favorite doll?"

"No. This is Mary. She's my second-favorite. I just finded her." She hugged her.

"Alice, please come and sit down next to Mommy," the woman said gently, but Alice seemed to have a mind of her own.

"She was lost and I finded her," Alice told Mattias, fascinated with him for some reason.

"Did you happen to see the people themselves? Even how they were dressed?" James asked, and the woman shook her head.

"These two keep me pretty busy. I only thought about it after I heard about the robbery. There was nothing suspicious at the time. I think they might have been there for about an hour, and then I didn't see the van anymore."

"All right, thank you," James said. There was no point in pushing her further. A relatively plain white work van. That seemed to be common in two of the reports. Another described a green minivan. She hadn't seen any more that day, and pressuring her wasn't likely to yield anything. "We appreciate you seeing us." He smiled and glanced at Mattias before standing and heading down the steps off the porch and out to the car.

"Alice, no!"

Frantic fear rang in the air. James turned as the little girl ran out into the street, a car coming down toward her. Mattias raced back across, grabbed Alice, and propelled them both to the sidewalk, the car passing with a blare of the horn.

Alice's mother raced out as Mattias held the girl. "Thank you… thank you," she said, taking Alice's hand. "You don't go into the street, you know that."

"But, Mommy," Alice said, pointing.

Mattias turned where she was pointing and walked back across the street and down slightly. "James," he called as he walked over. "Look there."

"It's an old toy," James said, shrugging his shoulders. "Like one of those Fisher-Price figures. I'll get a bag." He doubted it was meaningful, but he bagged the item and returned to the car, ready to go, but didn't see Mattias. He was back on the porch, kneeling down, talking to the little girl, who held her mom's hand but seemed to be answering. Then Mattias stood, ruffled Alice's hair, and hurried back over to the car. "You can give her the toy if it's hers."

Mattias slid into the passenger seat. "It isn't. Alice saw the van. She was interested in it because there was a kid. She saw him playing there. Alice said she wanted to give the boy the toy back in case it was his favorite." He buckled up.

"Wait…." James started the engine and stopped. "Do you think the thieves brought a kid with them?"

"It's possible. They pull up, go about their business, a kid playing nearby in the grass. The thieves get what they want, pack up, hustle the little boy into the van, and drive away, leaving the toy behind. Now granted, that toy could have been there for months, but it looks fairly fresh and isn't encrusted with dirt." Mattias held up the bag, looking at the red figure.

"Could it be that it fell out of the back?" James offered.

"Except Alice saw the boy. She wanted to go play with him and went to ask her mom, but they were gone when she came back. At least that's what I think she was trying to tell me. She said he dropped his toy. I know she's a four-year-old, but what if she did see our thieves, and what if this is their toy? Thieves have kids too," Mattias said.

James nodded. "I'm more than aware of that." He pulled away, gripping the wheel once more. "Bringing a kid to a crime." It was hard for him to get over, but then, he'd also seen some of the things parents did to their children, so why in the hell did this surprise him so damned much?

"I knew a woman who used her child as a distraction so she could steal jewelry." Mattias sighed and shook his head. "There's no such thing as a victimless crime." He sat quietly in his seat as James drove, contemplating the possibilities of what they had found.

"Do you think this is a family business?" James asked. The thought made his stomach roil, and he swallowed hard.

"I don't know. It's way too soon to tell, but at least we have a few more questions we can ask." Mattias grew quiet, and James was fine with that. The next witness was only a few minutes away, and he needed to get his head back in the game. They could worry about possibilities once they got back to the station. For now they needed to gather any information that they could.

UNFORTUNATELY, THE next witness had only seen much the same. A van, white, parked down the street in front of the victim's house. James asked about seeing people or children, but the older man shook his head. It might have been the same van, but that was about the only thing they were able to substantiate.

James and Mattias returned to the car and headed back to the station. The others hadn't returned his calls. James couldn't get over the idea of a kid being brought to a robbery. It unsettled him no end.

"Why would someone bring a kid to a crime?"

Mattias shrugged. "Look, I don't know. I would never do it. Aside from it being despicable, kids are unpredictable, and I always tried to control as many variables as I could." He shook his head. "But it looks like it's a possibility…."

"What are you thinking?" James asked as they rode along through the country between the towns, passing fields and occasional farmhouses.

"I don't know. It's probably nothing." Mattias shifted in his seat. "I keep thinking about what Alice saw. These thieves are pretty bold and confident if they are willing to bring kids to a job. Though I guess we don't know for sure that what Alice saw was one of the thieves. It was hard for me to get any more details from her. She's too young. Maybe it was a different van or a different day. It could have been a legitimate workman who was there for a short period and didn't have child-care." He sighed.

James nodded. All of that was possible. "What does your gut tell you? That doesn't hold up in court, but sometimes it's all we have to go on, at least to begin with." He sped up as the road stretched out in front of them. James wanted to get back to the station to check with the guys to see if they had had any better luck.

"It's telling me that Alice saw the thieves and a kid was with them," Mattias said. "I wish I knew the hell why, but I believe her. She wanted to go play with him, but Mommy had the door locked, and she could only watch through the window."

"Smart mama." Given what could have happened, a lucky mama as well. James would hate to be investigating the disappearance of that cute little girl, and that could have been possible if she'd interrupted something like a break-in. Sometimes James's mind went a little wild with possibilities, and he needed to rein it in. Otherwise, he knew he could go in circles and get nowhere.

His phone rang, and he answered it through the car. "Detective Levinson."

"Yes. I'm Clarence Fisher, and I received a message that you wanted to speak with me. The police were already here, but I will be home for the next hour."

"Thank you. We'll be there in—" James pulled over and looked through the notes he'd made. "—ten minutes tops. We're heading your way. Thank you for agreeing to meet with us." He ended the call and pulled back onto the road, heading to the west side of Carlisle, where expensive homes had been built where the old hospital had been torn down. He pulled up in front of the brick colonial, the lawn beautifully kept and bushes immaculately trimmed. Mattias and he traversed the slab bluestone walk and rang the bell.

"I'm over here," a man in his early fifties said, stepping off a small side porch. "Just follow on around."

"This is beautiful," Mattias said as they approached where the man sat in a faux-wicker chair.

"Thank you. I'm Clarence Fisher." He stood, and they took the seats he offered after James made introductions. "I've been trying to get the beds settled, but with all this rain, I haven't had a chance to get out here most days." He sat back and placed his hands on the arms of the chair. "What can I do for you fellows?"

"We understand that you might have seen the thieves who robbed your neighbors," James said. "I know you talked to the police already, but we're working across the county to try to catch these people."

"Well, yeah, I think I did see them. They were bold, I have to give you that. The Felders live right over there. I had taken the day off from work because it was sunny and I had to get something done. I was working over here when this van pulled up in front of the house. It was dark green, and two people got out in coveralls. They marched on up to the front door like they belonged. I didn't think much of it and continued working. After a little while, the van pulled around the back. That was when I lost sight of it. I figured they were having work done, but I should have known. Those houses are very new and shouldn't need a lot of work."

"Can you describe the people you saw in any detail?" James asked.

"They weren't very big. At first I thought they were women, but no. It was men. They walked like men, and from what I heard, they must have filled the van out of the back and then left. Most people are gone during the day, so they had plenty of time. Whoever did this really cased the place. They knew the Felders had a number of valuable items, and they cleaned them out. These weren't TV kind of thieves—they took the good stuff. Mrs. Felder is French, and she had a number of small, intricate antique pieces that were all taken."

Mattias leaned closer. "We understand that and are trying to use the descriptions to hunt down their property." James shot him a stern look, but Mattias came even nearer. "Were you here the entire time?"

"Yes. I should have gone over and taken a look. I could have called the police. Instead…." Clarence lowered his head.

"This wasn't your fault," Mattias told him gently. "This was the people who committed the crime, nothing more. I know you think you might have helped, but putting yourself in danger wasn't going to do you or them any good." He paused. "Are you sure about the color of the van?"

"Yes. It sat right over there. They aren't supposed to park on that side of the street, but they did anyway. I bet that's partly why they moved. But I remember it clearly because they were parked where they shouldn't be."

"Can you show us exactly where they parked?" Mattias asked.

Clarence stood and walked around the corner of the house. "Right beside that tree there." He pointed, and James nodded.

"Thank you for everything." He wished Mr. Fisher had more information for them, but he'd been helpful nonetheless.

Mattias was already on his way over to where Mr. Fisher had indicated. James followed him. "Anything interesting?"

"If I remember the files we went through, this robbery was a week ago. I know there isn't much chance that anything remains of their presence, but I thought it might be worth a look."

James rolled his eyes. "Carlisle PD has been over this with a fine-tooth comb."

"I bet they have." Mattias knelt down and ran his hands over the grass. "I'm not questioning that." He stood, looking at the house. "This place is a thief's paradise. They parked the van right here, largely blocking the view of the front door and porch. That gave them time to pick the lock and get in. Once they're inside, they have the run of the place. No alarm, and it's during the day." James stepped back, looking up and down the street. "It's probably easier to hit homes in this neighborhood during the day than night. Everyone is home then."

"You're so sure about that?"

"Yeah. They were inside the house for probably half an hour, gathering what they could easily take and putting it by the back door." Mattias stepped around to the side of the house and then came out in back on the alley. "I bet they parked here, with the side door open to the yard, the van blocking the view again. They loaded up, closed the door, got in, and were gone, just like that." He wandered around, running his fingers over some rocks.

"What?"

"The van is leaking oil," Mattias said.

"How do you know? It could be one of the owners' cars." James was ready to go and get back so he could follow up on what the other guys were looking into. This was turning out to be a fool's errand that had yielded almost nothing.

"Look at the spatters. We've had rain, so they aren't as clear, but the drips go across the drive instead of into the garage. I bet they pulled up slowly to stop and left this trail of oil. Then the van dripped here for a while before they left." Mattias stood. "I bet they didn't get very far. It was a pretty bad leak."

"So…." James huffed.

"Check the garages and repair shops in town. Someone towed it, and my guess is they are sitting on a van that they will never see the owner of again." Mattias smiled. "Maybe if we can find it, the van will tell us something." He turned and strode back to the car as though he had just made a pronouncement of epic proportions. "Are you ready to go?"

James rolled his eyes. This guy was annoying on top of frustrating. "You're a real pain in the ass, you know that?" he hissed when he caught up. "There's no need to be a know-it-all."

"I have to prove that my insight is worth something," Mattias explained, then stopped by the car. "I know you don't think very highly of my skills, but I'm trying to be helpful to the investigation."

"Then drop the attitude." James pulled open his door.

"I will if you will," Mattias countered with a wicked grin, and damn it all, James found it difficult to be angry with the guy. "We could both drop the attitude and just try to work together."

James had to get over this fascination with Mattias. Yeah, he was covering up his attraction with sarcasm and impatience. Instead, he needed to be part of the team, if only for Solly's sake.

As they rode back to the station, James made a few calls. "Did you find anything by talking with the victims?" James asked Pierre.

"Not much. They all seemed to know how they got in, and they all felt as though they were targeted and probably staked out for what they had."

"Do they have anything in common?" Mattias asked. "Our thieves may be stalking neighborhoods, but that seems too random to me."

James hummed and nodded. That sounded logical.

"What sort of things?" Pierre inquired.

"I don't know. But you met with some of them— did they go to the same club or play golf? Maybe they have the same interests. Do they all… I don't know… use the same gym? There must be something that is helping the thieves." Mattias grew quiet, and James took over.

"Take everything you have and plug it into the spreadsheet Mattias shared with us. Don't speculate, but fill in as much information as you can, and have Clay do the same when he gets back. We're on our way in now, and we can review things before calling it a day." James ended the call and meandered through town with its myriad of lights until he managed to get through and then out to the station.

"Do you have any ideas?" Mattias asked.

"Not yet. But I think you're right. We're going to have to put together everything we possibly can in order to come up with a solution."

Mattias's phone rang. "Yes."

James didn't want to eavesdrop as he parked and then opened his door.

"You have to be kidding me." Mattias got out, huffing and looking upward. "A cow. Fine, cancel my stay and I'll call around and see if I can find another place…." Mattias listened and then rolled his eyes. "Of course they are. Well, I'll have to figure something out. Thank you." Mattias hung up and jabbed his phone into his pocket.

"Anything wrong?"

"When I was contracted here, the only hotel I could get was one outside of town by the turnpike— everything else was booked. That side of town doesn't have power right now. A farmer buried a cow and cut the major trunk line for that area. And apparently the hotels are all full because of a huge auto show at the fairgrounds, so I have to try to find a place." They headed inside the station. "I'll figure something out."

CHAPTER 3

MATTIAS FOUND an old sofa in the changing area, and after retrieving his things from the hotel and making use of the available rudimentary facilities, he turned off most of the lights and lay down, pulling a light jacket over his shoulders. It was late, and there were no hotel rooms available, between the car show and the power outage, which extended across the east side of town. Not that it mattered, really. He had slept on worse, and it was only for one night. Tomorrow, hopefully, his hotel would have power back and he could return to his room. He closed his eyes and let fatigue wash over him. At least he tried, but ended up rolling over again and again as he tried to find a position that was comfortable.

After a few minutes of lying on his side, a position that seemed okay, an unpleasant scent from the sofa lightly tickled his nose and only grew stronger. He sat up with a groan and shook his head.

"Are you still here?" James asked as he came in. "I figured you had left a while ago."

"I thought the same about you." Mattias stood, stretching his back. "If you want suspects to talk, just give them this thing to sleep on. They'll spill national secrets." He rubbed his lower back and snatched up his jacket.

"No hotel?" James asked. "I understand one of the main electric lines is out."

"Yeah. I got my things in case it doesn't come on, but every room for miles is booked up. We had work to do, so I put it off, and now… it looks like Old Stinky and I are going to make a night of it." He wasn't looking forward to it.

"Come on. I had some paperwork I needed to finish for my captain. It's done and he has it, so why don't you head out with me? I have a guest room, and you can stay there until you can get a hotel room."

"You don't have to do that," Mattias said. He wasn't looking for pity. Mattias had learned how to take care of himself a long time ago.

"Solly said we were to be a team, and if that's true, then we need to help each other." James grabbed Mattias's bag off the floor. "Besides, I think after a night on that thing, you'd be in no shape to help anyone." He pulled open the changing area door.

Mattias was desperate enough that he followed quietly behind. His back eased in utter relief, and his nose was eternally grateful to be away from that smell.

It was nearly dark as they stepped outside. "Do you want me to follow you?"

"No need. Ride with me. We're coming to the same place in the morning," James said, and Mattias was too tired to argue or snark at him. He just got into the car and buckled himself in, relieved he was going to have a bed for the evening. James put his bag in the trunk.

"Thanks for doing this," Mattias said as James got in the car.

"The ride is going to take a little while. I live close to the first witness that we spoke to." He pulled out and made the turn, heading to the main road.

Mattias wasn't familiar with the area and had used GPS to get to the station, so he sat back and let James do the driving. Silence lingered between them, and Mattias tried to think of something to bring up, anything to fill the quiet in the car. Normally he was a huge fan of quiet, but being with James only made him wonder what he was thinking.

"Have you been to this area before?"

"Once, some time ago," Mattias said.

James looked over at him, his eyes flashing with reflected light. Mattias could almost feel his curiosity bubbling up. "Was this in your previous profession?"

Mattias should have expected that. "No. I was a kid, and my grandparents brought me up here one week. We went camping at Kings Gap. Poppy and Nana rented an RV, and we spent the week. I went swimming, and I remember nothing but happiness. Those were the good times before the foster homes and such." Mattias kept the welling sadness out of his voice.

"I see," James said with an odd tone that Mattias couldn't read. Mattias knew there was no way that James could possibly understand, and he figured it was better to leave it at the simple explanation rather than the one that could take some time.

He shook his head. "I had a childhood. I didn't come out of my mother's womb and decide to steal the buttons off her shirt. All that came later, out of necessity." Mattias shook his head. "Is this self-righteousness an attitude, or do you bathe in it?"

"I didn't say anything," James said, but it was clear enough to Mattias that the attitude was there.

He needed to let go of chip he carried, but James got him all stirred up. "I appreciate you letting me stay at your house. And for the record, you don't need to worry about me stealing your silver or pinching your mother's jewelry. I don't steal for a living any longer. With me it isn't a compulsion. It was a means to make a living… nothing more."

James nodded. "I know. You made a living out of the misery of others."

"For your information, I had plenty of misery in my life. Heaps of it. I didn't have a way to make a living, so I learned. It was survival, and I found out I was good at it." Mattias paused a second. "I'm no Robin Hood, but neither am I the man who robs their neighbor who had less than they do in order to buy drugs. It was a profession, and I made a living at it for a number of years. I'm up front about it, and in a way, I'm working with departments like Solly's to help make up for the things I did." He glared at James, meeting his gaze with as much fire as he could muster. "I won't apologize for what I had to do. I can't…. I survived and came out the other side." He heaved for breath as piles of vitriol came out. Mattias had no idea where all of this was coming from. He was normally a relatively quiet, thoughtful guy who helped police departments understand thieves and catch them. His job was generally to stay in the background, support the police officers, and help them do their jobs better. With James, it was completely different. "Maybe this wasn't such a good idea."

James scoffed. "What? You can't take a little heat?"

"Heat, yes. Know-it-all hatred I can do without." Mattias rolled his eyes, looking out the window because he needed to watch something, anything, other than James and his intense brown gaze that fluttered his belly each time he looked into it. This was a really bad thought, and Mattias got the idea that it was only going to get worse. Still, he couldn't very well ask James to take him back to the station so he could sleep on Old Stinky.

"I don't know it all," James said with less power behind the words. "Lord knows if I claimed that, lightning would strike me dead in an instant." He slowed as they came into town, passing through a commercial main street before turning off. James pulled up in front of a small row house and put the car in Park. Mattias got out, inhaling the warm, humid air, and got his bag when James popped open the trunk. Then he went with James to the narrowest row house he had ever seen. It couldn't have been more than ten or twelve feet wide.

"This is where you live?" Mattias asked.

"Yeah. My grandparents lived here for forty years, and when my grandmother passed, she left it to me." James unlocked the door, and Mattias followed him inside. "My grandfather remodeled it, and he opened the stairs to add more space to the front room." James dropped his keys into a bowl and locked the door behind them. It was largely a shotgun house, with one room leading to the next, living room, dining room, kitchen, and then the bedrooms upstairs. The decorating was simple, with honey-oak floors, plain rugs, and cool, subdued colors on the walls.

"It's very nice." Mattias smiled as the décor soothed him. It really was so pleasant and not at all what he had expected. He'd pictured a big, manly house with huge, dark, masculine furniture, dripping with testosterone, all positioned in front of a huge television set the size of Montana. Not that there was anything wrong with that at all. Mattias loved a man cave. But this was warm and inviting, and it lightened his spirit, though Mattias couldn't quite figure out why. He trailed his hand along the back of one of the chairs.

"Most of the furniture was my grandmother's. I had it all re-covered. It was in great shape, but the fabric was worn out." James set down his bag. "Have a seat. I'm going to get something heating up to eat. Then I can show you the guest room and stuff." James hurried away, and Mattias sat down, yawning as he got comfortable, glancing around the room to check out James's clean but warm taste in furnishings. His stomach rumbled, but he figured it was best to stay out of James's way.

"Come on," James said as he breezed into the room.

Mattias hefted himself out of the chair and headed upstairs behind James, enjoying the amazing view as they climbed. Man, James must have spent plenty of time on a StairMaster. Mattias was willing to bet he could bounce a quarter off those glutes.

"The guest room is the one right in the front of the house." James pushed open the door, and Mattias stepped into a calming room with light gray walls and white furniture. The main pop of color was a sky-blue comforter on the bed. "Go ahead and get comfortable. The bathroom is the next door down. I'm going to finish some dinner. Meet you in the kitchen." James took off fast.

Mattias set his bag off to the side, sat on the edge of the bed, and then lay back, letting the perfect mattress cradle him, a sigh escaping as he closed his eyes. This was a lot better than that damned sofa, or even the hotel room. This felt like a home, a real home. He tried to remember the last time he'd felt this way, and it was difficult. He went back, allowing his mind to take the trip through time. Then he smiled as his nana tucked him in and told him a story as Mattias listened, taking in every word. Those times had been simple and perfect, something he'd thought would never end.

Suddenly Mattias sat up, wiping his eyes, pushing away the images. Dwelling on them and what came afterward wasn't productive in the least. He stood and made a stop in the bathroom before descending the stairs and going to find James. Maybe some snark and sarcasm would banish those memories for a while.

"Are you hungry?" James motioned him to the small table and set a bowl of steaming pasta and sauce in front of him. "It isn't the greatest. I had to start with jarred sauce, but I doctored it up, and the stuff isn't too bad." He brought over a second bowl, setting it at his own place. "I have some wine if you want it." James poured himself a glass and then one for Mattias after he nodded.

"Smells good," Mattias said, and took his first bite. The sauce had zip and a touch of heat. It was awesome, and Mattias ate faster as his appetite kicked in full force.

"I generally make some things on my day off that I can heat up when I get home." James sipped his wine and swirled some of the pasta around his fork. "I have to ask. Do you work on a lot of cases like ours?"

"I have," Mattias answered. "Thieves have a number of things in common. First and foremost, they don't want to get caught, but eventually most of them overreach. They believe that one big score is going to make all their dreams come true. They case expensive houses and break in, triggering alarms, or they steal things that can be traced. A lot of expensive gems and items are actually microtagged with serial numbers so they can be found if stolen. Insurance companies have detailed lists of jewelry and other items, sometimes complete with pictures, so they can be located pretty fast. The last thing they want to do is pay out for a hugely expensive item unless they can help it."

"So you work with a lot of insurance companies?" James asked, lightly tapping his fingers on the tabletop.

Mattias swallowed and took a sip of the nice wine, nodding slowly. "They were some of my first clients. Insurance companies are pretty mercenary. They really don't care how an item gets returned as long as they don't have to pay out." He took another small bite of pasta. "One of my first jobs was the recovery of a small block print that had been stolen. It was a Dürer and was heavily insured. The thieves had broken in, taken a number of items, and thought that the print might be valuable, so they stole it too." Mattias shook his head. "That was their first mistake. The theft made news because of what was taken, and the print was suddenly a huge liability. They were going to have a hard time selling it, and they couldn't be caught with it in their possession."

"How did you get it back?"

"I scoured online auction records and found a listing for an auction house on the other side of the country. They were selling the print there. The thieves had grown impatient and figured distance would work for them. It took six months, but with the help of the auction house, we let the item go to sale. It was only for show, though. The auction house told the sellers that they needed to come in to collect the check because there was an issue with the paperwork. The police took the man into custody, and he gave up the other people he worked with." Mattias finished the pasta and sat back. "Sometimes it takes patience. The Mona Lisa was gone for two years when it was stolen, and some things are missing for a decade, but they can be returned."

"Uh-huh. You know that the more time passes, the less chance there is of that," James pronounced.

Mattias couldn't argue with that. "Yes. But sometimes it takes some patience for things to reappear. The old adage of lying low for a while kicks in, but then impatience starts to take its toll. That's what happened with the block print. It was recovered. The insurance money wasn't paid out, and the family got their artwork back... eventually... along with a few other of their items." Mattias shrugged. He was pretty sure that James had heard stories like that one before. "After that, I was asked to consult on other cases, and then police departments brought me in. And the rest, as they say, is history."

"How long before that did you give up the business?" James asked, wriggling his fingers.

Mattias rolled his eyes and decided to let the "light fingers" reference pass. "A good year. I had plenty of money and was secure. I didn't want to be one of those people who stole their entire lives and ended up in jail at forty. And it was time to make a change in my life. So I decided to go legitimate, and I guess I got lucky." He drank the last of his wine. "This is really nice." He set down the glass. "Thank you for the dinner and the wine, as well as the place to sleep. I really appreciate it." It was pleasant not sniping at each other... at least for now. "Why law enforcement? Is it a family business?"

James threw back the last of his wine as though it were a shot of whiskey. "No. I decided when I was a kid that I wanted to be a police officer. I've always known it was what I wanted to do. After high school, I put myself through college, majored in criminal justice, and then went through the academy. I started in Philadelphia for a while, but wanted a smaller town, so I got a job here in Mechanicsburg. Solly and I were roommates for a couple of years, but he always knew he was going to return here. This area is where he grew up." James stood and grabbed the wine bottle to refill both glasses. It seemed that the sharing period of the evening was over, which was fine with Mattias. He'd managed to open up a little without going into the gory details of his past, and if James wasn't up to sharing, then he could respect that. "How did you get this gig with Solly?"

"I worked with the Philadelphia property crime division six months ago, and they brought me into one of the regional law enforcement gatherings. Sheriff Briggs was at the gathering, and he invited me here." Mattias got up and took his dish and silverware to the sink, then returned to the table and sat back down. His grandmother would roll over in her grave if he wasn't a good guest. "I know you can investigate crime, but the sheriff felt that there was something else going on here and figured some support was warranted." Mattias thought it was best not to impugn the local police expertise.

"What do you think is different?" James rested his arms on the table.

"I have a couple of theories. The first is that this is a group that moved into the area a few months ago. They stake out their victims, go in, do the jobs, and get out. As soon as we turn up the heat, they'll move on and go somewhere else." Mattias met James's intense gaze. "Sort of a traveling band of burglars. I've met some of these people, and you don't want to cross them. They've done this sort of thing for a while, and they get in and out fast." Mattias paused to think. "But I doubt that's the case this time. Professionals would have new equipment, a business name professionally painted on the side of the vehicle, and their van wouldn't pee oil all over the driveway. That would leave too much of a presence behind. Those folks are like ghosts, and they don't stay very long once the jobs are done. In and out of the houses, and the area."

"I agree with that. A well-financed group would be just like you said. They'd even have a phone number on the van that would be active. Maybe just an answering machine, but something to throw off suspicion." James smiled slightly. "So what's your next theory?"

"Homegrown thieves who organized. Most likely they have someone organizing them." Mattias raised his gaze. "There could even be more than one group, which would explain the different-colored vans, or maybe the one died and they replaced it. I bet the witnesses did see the thieves' vehicles, and the reason they saw different-colored ones is because there is more than one." He nodded as a picture began forming in his mind.

"A local version of organized crime?" James asked.

"Or it was put together by one of the gangs or crime organizations. It's hard to say. This area has enough people who are desperate and hanging on by a thread. Now imagine the chance to make some real money fast. It's the same lure as the drug trade." Mattias sighed. "People don't just do this to do it. It's dangerous. You can get caught, or killed by a neighbor or law enforcement if they happen upon you and believe you're a danger to them. You are on someone else's property, and you have no right to be there. But when people get desperate, they will do just about anything." He nodded and waited for James to contradict him or present his own opinion, but he stayed quiet.

"What do you suggest we do?" James asked, which surprised him a little.

"We have to start with good police work. That's where you come in. I'm only here to help and try to provide any insight that I can. There's a pattern to all of this, and we need to look closer until we find it. That's the one way to catch these folks. We can wait for them to make a mistake, but by then more people will be robbed." Mattias knew he wasn't telling James anything he didn't know, and their conversation fell off.

James finished his wine and brought in the newspaper, setting it on the table. He took the front section and pushed the rest of it to the center of the table, and Mattias grabbed the What's Happening section.

"There are a couple of charity events, and...." Mattias spread out the paper to read it and then lifted his gaze once James had closed his section. "What's a house tour?"

"Some of the groups in town put together home tours to raise money." James's eyes widened.

"And it's an excellent way for people to case a number of homes, and no one would be the wiser." Mattias passed over the page with the article. "Our thieves buy tickets and get to go through ten nicely decorated, pristine homes that the owners are very proud of... to case the joints." He understood why it was a fund-raiser, but the danger was also very real. If he were one of these thieves, he'd certainly buy a ticket.

"Do we ask them to cancel it? The historical society is running this one. They normally do one at Christmas, but this is a special one of the most historic homes." James set the paper aside.

"I think we need to contact them and maybe volunteer—watch people and see if there is anyone who doesn't fit the profile of their customer. It's a long shot, but we can give it a try. It's Saturday from two until five. It's only three hours. Talk to one of the guys who lives in Carlisle and see if they know anyone who can get us in." Mattias took back the paper and pointed to another article. "There's also the benefit for the theater. It looks like that is going to draw a crowd of some of the most well-heeled in town. Another chance for them to watch people and find potential victims." He sat back and finished the last of his wine. "I'll go ahead and swing two tickets for that."

"How?" James looked over the paper. "Aren't they pretty expensive?"

Mattias nodded. "I can handle those tickets. You manage the arrangements for the house tour, and we'll be all set." He stood and put his glass in the sink. "If it's okay, I'm going to go up to bed. It's getting late, and we have plenty to do in the morning." Mattias headed out of the room and stopped. "By the way, the theater benefit is black-tie. Do you have a tuxedo?" He wagged his eyebrows, because he was sure that James in a tux would be stunning, and it would be more than worth the price of two benefit tickets to see that.

James growled—the man actually growled—and Mattias paused. He had been teasing him. Mattias hadn't wanted to make him truly angry.

"We don't all live like James Bond."

"I don't either," Mattias snapped and forced himself to calm down. "I don't have a tuxedo here with me either. Don't worry. I'll get the tickets, and then we'll arrange for the clothes. It's no problem."

"I could just wear my dress uniform," James offered, and Mattias waited for him to think about that more clearly. "Yeah… okay… that would defeat the purpose, wouldn't it?"

"Yes. Like I said, don't worry about it. I did some work for a friend a few years ago who has a formal-wear shop on Carlisle Pike. If you can get up there, I'm sure he'll be able to help us out." Mattias patted the doorframe and stifled a yawn. "I really need to try to get some sleep." He was dead on his feet, and fatigue was catching up with him a lot quicker than he wanted to admit.

"I'll go up with you." James rinsed the dishes and then turned out the lights. They walked through the rooms and then up the stairs. "I have fresh towels in the bathroom for you, and if you need more, they're in the closet in there. I'll see you in the morning." James lingered in the hallway, and Mattias wondered if it was because of his trust issues. Mattias went into the bedroom, closed the door, and got ready for bed, wondering just what he'd gotten himself in for with this assignment.

MATTIAS WOKE to a strange sound beneath him—whispers and a slight scrape. He pushed back the covers and sat up, listened as he got out of bed, and pulled open the bedroom door. James's door was still closed, but Mattias paid little attention, descending the stairs on his thief's catlike feet as the scrape came again. Someone was trying to get into the house using the front door. As he drew closer, one of the old floorboards squeaked. He cringed and held still, but the sound stopped. Mattias veered into the living room, peering out into the night. A dark van was parked right in front of the house, blocking the view of the front door.

"What are you doing?" James asked as he lumped down the stairs.

Mattias didn't turn away as figures bolted from in front of the house. Doors opened and closed, and the van pulled away within seconds. "Trying to catch our thieves," Mattias said as he let the curtain rest back into place.

"What?" James wiped his eyes, and Mattias blinked. James in his boxer shorts was a glorious sight, all muscle and richly tanned skin with a dusting of dark hair over his pecs and down his belly.

"I'm a light sleeper. I heard a slight scraping sound, and I came down here to check it out. There was a van parked in front, and I was trying to see if I could make out anything special about it." Mattias swallowed as James reached for the door. "I suggest you put on more than just those striped shorts or you'll be giving the entire neighborhood something to look at." He smirked, and James blushed high on his cheeks. He turned and hurried back up the stairs. At least Mattias was in a pair of shorts and a T-shirt.

He waited for James to return and let him open the door, turning on lights. "I need to get some gloves." James hurried away again, and Mattias looked over the lock without touching it.

"They were trying to pick it and not doing a very good job," Mattias said when James returned, doing his best not to keep looking over at the way his dark T-shirt stretched over his chest. Damn, the man would look good in a plastic garbage bag. Mattias pulled his attention back to the task at hand. "It's possible they got past the door lock, but the dead bolt was proving to be more difficult." He backed away so James could get closer, stepping outside into the illumination from the streetlamp. The van would have blocked the light and the view of the front door. "They really hurt themselves."

"How so?" James asked as he examined the lock further.

"They parked their van to block the view, but it also made it harder for them to work. They would have needed flashlights, but those could draw attention." Mattias pointed to a small penlight next to the steps. "Looks like they dropped something." He didn't touch anything, but looked up and down the street. "Why you?" Mattias asked. The house was smaller than the others, and there was nothing remarkable about it. "Did you draw attention to yourself somehow?" As soon as the words escaped his lips, he shook his head. Of course not. James was all about work. Mattias knelt down, watching as James gathered what evidence there was. "Why would anyone try to break into your house?"

"It's happened before," James mumbled.

"Excuse me?" Mattias asked. "You're a cop. Doesn't that scare the crap out of them?" Hell, it would him if he were still in the business. What surprised Mattias the most was how calm James was. People had tried to break into his house before? Shit, no wonder he'd been antagonistic.

James stepped back from the door and motioned for Mattias to come inside. He closed the door, locked it, and made a phone call, probably waking up one of the guys. "Clay will be here in the morning to look over anything I might have missed." He set the plastic bag on the table and sank into one of the chairs.

Mattias took a seat near him. "What's going on? What is it I'm missing?" This made no sense. If people were trying to break into his house on a regular basis, he'd have moved a long time ago.

James sighed. "This is one of the oldest houses in town, and apparently there is an old story about one of the men who lived here before my family. Supposedly he was afraid of banks, so he hid money in the house and then died. In the time I've lived here, there have been two attempted break-ins, and one person who I met coming up the basement stairs after he spent half the night digging up the floor." James shivered. "I don't know who was more scared, but I'm willing to bet it was him when he saw I had a gun pointed at him and was ready to shoot. The idiot." Now some of the anger Mattias had expected from James came to the surface. "After that, I changed the locks. Ordered special ones from Europe that take keys that aren't available here in the US." He got up, grabbed his ring of keys from the bowl, and showed Mattias a strangely angled two-prong key. "They can try to pick that deadbolt until they're blue in the face, but it isn't happening. The deadbolt slot is anchored into the house itself, not just into the doorframe. So, try as they might, they weren't getting in."

Mattias nodded and then shook his head. "I'm glad that you're safe and protected." He reached for the ring, examined the key, and then handed it back.

"Do you think you could pick it?" James asked.

"Probably not. I could probably get past the lock with enough preparation, but it would be difficult. Not impossible." Mattias didn't move, even as his head ran through possibilities. "I'd probably need to take an impression of the key and then have one made. The process would take time, be expensive, and probably yield me a key that didn't really work after all, because I'm assuming the lock is highly sensitive." He sighed.

"Do you ever turn off that part of you?" James asked.

Mattias glared at him even as he pondered the question, and the answer was no. "You asked, I told you. And I was honest." He hoisted himself to his feet. "Sometimes you can be the biggest pain in the ass of anyone I have ever met. No lock is unbreakable, but this one makes getting in here not worth the effort. And that's probably the best defense you can have." He turned to leave the room and then stopped. "I love puzzles, always have. I think stealing things was like a puzzle for me. I'd work out how to get past the obstacles to get what I wanted. Then when I did it, I moved on to the next one."

He left the room and headed up the stairs, realizing that James Levinson was probably the biggest and most complex puzzle he had come across in years. The question was, did he want to try to solve him or just step back and leave him alone? Some puzzles were better unsolved; he knew that. But James was just too good to pass up.

CHAPTER 4

DAMN IT all. James needed to get some sleep, but
now he lay awake, staring at his recently painted ceiling, listening and wondering. His mind raced from
the people who tried to break in, to Mattias sleeping
in the other room. Yeah, Mattias hadn't gone around
the house flashing him the way James had apparently done, but his shorts were thin enough to leave very
little to the imagination. And that T-shirt—"Grass, it's
what's for dinner," with a cow on it—had been cute, but
the way it clung to Mattias's arms and chest had been
mouthwatering.

He shook his head, and the attempted break-in returned to his mind and he listened once more. He wasn't
going to get back to sleep. When his head got like this,
there was no use fighting it. James pushed back the
covers, grabbed a light blanket, and went downstairs.
He settled on the couch, found an old movie on demand, and settled in to watch.

James must have fallen asleep. He sat up, noticing
that the television was off, and then realized that Mattias was seated right across from him.

"I made coffee. I hope that's okay." He handed
James a mug.

"What time is it?" James sipped and blinked.

"A little after seven. I didn't want to wake you, but it's getting late."

James stood and took the mug. "I'll get ready and be back down here in ten minutes." He hurried up the stairs and right into the bathroom. He washed and shaved, jumped into the shower, and then hurried to the bedroom to dry off and dress. James made it downstairs and put his mug in the sink, loaded the dishwasher, and then met Mattias in the living room.

"Is that what you're going to wear?" Mattias asked.

"Why?" James headed for the door.

"You're wearing two different shoes," Mattias said.

James glanced down, swearing under his breath. He went back upstairs, changed his shoes, and met Mattias by the front door.

"You know, you could have started a whole new fashion trend."

"Don't start this morning, okay? I didn't sleep very well last night." The doorbell rang, and James groaned, hurrying outside to the front, where Clay stood. James had forgotten that he'd asked him to come over. His mind was all over the place this morning.

"Just take care of things," Mattias said, and sat down.

James took Clay out, and they worked the scene now that they could see more clearly.

"What's going on? He's staying with you?" Clay asked. "I thought you didn't like the guy." Clay examined the lock and pulled out a kit to check for fingerprints.

"The power outage," James answered, as though that explained everything. He didn't want to talk about

Mattias because that would only allow his confusion around the guy to bubble to the surface again, and it had been there all night. "Mattias saw the van. It matches some of the descriptions of the people we are after."

Clay worked the rest of the area, including where James told him the van had been parked. There were a few things that he bagged, but mostly they had gotten everything the night before, most of it probably useless, and the area was clean. "So our thieves decided it would be a good idea to try to break into the house of the detective in charge of the case," Clay scoffed, his eyebrows knitting together. "That has to be a coincidence."

James wished he could say that it was. The story about the treasure that he'd told Mattias was a smoke screen of sorts. What he'd said was true and it had all happened, but James didn't think that had anything to do with the rash of thieves or why his house was targeted last night. "I don't think so." He lifted his gaze to Clay's.

"You think they targeted you on purpose?" Clay's eyes widened, and he leaned just a little closer. "Really? Are they the stupidest criminals in history? Maybe they should be permanent guests on *Stupid Criminal Tricks*." He flashed a quick smile.

"No. I think I'm being sent a message." The idea sent a chill racing into James's gut. It made him angrier than he could have ever imagined, but it was true.

Clay stood, holding two evidence bags, and placed them in the evidence container. Then he returned to the work of lifting the prints. "How could anyone have known that you would be on the case so fast? I know word gets out on the street and all, and groups watch. But we all just started working it yesterday. And why would they want to send you a message? To get you to back off? Like that's going to happen." He continued working as James paced the front of the house, looking for something, anything, that leaped out at him that they might have missed. His head spun, and he clenched his hands into fists.

James waited until Clay had finished, grateful that he had let the conversation end. By the time he was done, James had sent him the pictures he'd taken the night before with everything he'd found, and then they returned inside. James showed Clay what he had gathered last night and helped him label each of the bags. When they were done, Clay left with everything, and James returned to the living room.

"Let's go." He didn't say anything more as they left, locked the door, and headed to the station to go to work. This entire situation was getting under his skin, and James needed to leave as much of it behind as possible. He had a job to do, and no messages sent in the middle of the night were going to stop him from doing it. Hell, he'd send a message of his own, and it was going to be one that ended in their prosecution.

"OKAY, WHAT do we have?" James asked the room as he wandered through. Anxiety built inside him, and he had no idea why. He'd lived with pressure his entire life, but at the moment, he was like a nervous cat and couldn't sit still.

"I'm not sure," Mattias answered, and James didn't smile.

"I need coffee," Pierre said, scraping his chair on the floor and then leaving the room. Clay followed, both of them rigid, with the door closing behind them.

"Well…." Mattias looked up from his screen. "Where's the snide comment?" He sat back, his arms out as though he were some prisoner waiting for the fatal blow.

James shook his head. "You can't find a pattern either?"

Mattias sat back up. "No, and it's driving me crazy. I know there's one here. I just can't quite figure it out." He gaped a second, his mouth open. "Duh…."

"What?" James asked.

"There isn't a pattern because there's more than one group." Mattias continued staring at the screen and motioned James over.

James reluctantly drew nearer, and the temperature rose noticeably. He tugged at his collar and took off his jacket. Being near Mattias was like getting close to an erupting volcano. At least as far as he was concerned.

"Look, I concentrated on the vans for one thing. Some accounts say green and others white. Those aren't colors people confuse, and there are multiple accounts of both. I thought after the oil thing that maybe they had ditched the green one and gotten the white one, but it was around before that house was hit."

"So, two vans," James said with a nod. That made a lot of sense with what they had. "Maybe two groups of thieves… two teams…." That sent a chill running up James's spine.

Mattias turned, looking up at him with his huge, almost puppy-dog eyes. "This means that whoever is doing this has one hell of an organization behind them. I'm not going to say organized crime, because they don't seem that ruthless, but they have a team. It wouldn't take but five or six people to get together and form a team. They would have one or two people inside, another acting as a driver and lookout, and they could be all set to go." Mattias scratched the back of his head.

"We know that the green van team tried to break into my house, because you were smart enough to try to see them. Did you add that to the sheet?" James backed away. "It may not be exact, but look through and label the ones we know as white or green. Then maybe we can get a feel for them." He paused in his movements.

"Good idea," Mattias said, and returned to work. When he was done, he motioned James over. "Look at these...."

James leaned over his shoulder, trying to ignore the fresh scent that tickled his nose, like it was crooking a finger to try to get James to come in closer, just to get another whiff.

The others returned with extra cups of coffee, placed them on the table, and joined the group.

"It looks partially as though it's divided geographically, with the white van in Carlisle and the green van farther east. But there are exceptions, here and here. Maybe they overlap somewhat."

"Okay. We're starting to get a picture now," James said with relief. "We need to let law enforcement know what we have so far. At least officers can be on the lookout for suspicious vans meeting the descriptions that we have."

"I'm on it," Clay said, and left the room.

"What about this? Look at what was taken by this group. Someone here really likes antique pieces. There are a number of them taken here and almost none by the white van group," Pierre mentioned as he pointed.

"That could be meaningful. And that's the group from Carlisle. I'm willing to bet that they have someone with some knowledge or interest," James said.

"And that could be their weakness. If they're stealing these items, then they need to move them. I doubt they're just sitting on them, because the others will want their share." Mattias turned to James, who nodded.

"A lot of these items are going to be hard to trace, but a few are going to be relatively easy." James hooked the laptop up to the printer. "I did my best to get approximate pictures of them from the internet. The Queen Victoria locket is going to look like this." He showed it to them and then printed off copies. "I suggest you check local auction houses and antique shops to see if they have been approached. There are stores in Camp Hill, as well as Mechanicsburg, that specifically carry estate jewelry. Maybe we'll get lucky."

Clay and Pierre divided the work and returned to their desks.

"I think we need to visit these stores. See if they have been approached. We can probably do it in a few hours."

"Okay." Mattias packed up his laptop and slipped it into his case. "I'm going to bring this along. We can show them the actual images. It will help a lot more than just descriptions. Maybe something will jog some memories." He turned once he was ready, and the intensity in Mattias's gaze held James still for a few seconds. Mattias parted his lips, his eyes wide, meeting James's gaze full on. "Is something wrong?" Mattias asked after a few seconds, and James came out of the flight of intense, passionate fantasy that his mind had whisked him away on.

What the hell was wrong with him? James never had trouble concentrating at work, but with Mattias around, he couldn't seem to keep his head where it belonged. Instead of thinking about the case, he wondered how those supple lips would feel against his.

"I'm fine," he answered quickly, got his things, and turned to leave the suddenly confining space of the conference room.

THE COMBINATION antique and jewelry store was on the main street of Camp Hill, about twenty miles from Carlisle. The building was relatively new, modern brick. James parked and got out, thankful he could breathe now. The entire way he'd had the fan cranked to keep the air flowing and the tight quarters inside the car from overpowering him. He'd grown cold near the end of the trip, but ignored it. "Let me do the talking."

Mattias stopped on the sidewalk. "This is my expertise. Let me try first." He turned and breezed up to the door, practically flouncing inside the store.

James rolled his eyes and wondered what Mattias was up to, but figured he'd give him a little rope. Maybe he'd metaphorically hang himself with it and James could go back to normal.

"Good morning," Mattias said excitedly in response to the lady behind the counter. He clapped his hands together as he looked over the case in front of her. "You have amazing things."

"Well, thank you," she said, standing a little straighter. "Is there anything I can help you find?"

"I don't know. He and I were just out, and we saw your shop, and I just had to stop." Mattias flashed a huge smile as he continued to look inside one case and then moved on to the next. James did the same, peeking into the cases. Then he wandered through the store, glancing at each of the items for sale, trying to determine if any of them fit the various bulletins. So many things came across as alerts that it was impossible to commit all of them to memory, but there was always the chance something would stick out.

"Can I see that piece? It's absolutely gorgeous," Mattias asked, and James wandered back over.

"It's an engagement ring from the forties. It's just lovely, and we got it the other day. You're one of the first people to ask to see it," the saleslady said.

Mattias pulled out his phone. "Is it okay if I take a picture? My mom had one just that style, and she gave it up. You know how things can get when you retire. I want to see if it's close so I can replace it for her." Mattias took a picture and then moved back.

James's phone chimed with the picture and he wandered away to call Pierre. "I'm sending you a picture. It's a ring we think could be one that was stolen. Go through the spreadsheet, find the victim who lost an engagement ring, circa 1940, and contact her. See if this is hers and message me back." He put the phone in his pocket and rejoined Mattias, his heart pounding a little faster. There were few things as good as getting a lead, other than actually returning someone's stolen property.

Mattias thanked her, and the lady put the ring back. Then he wandered through the store, continuing to look at the various cases and displays. "Have you heard back?" Mattias asked quietly.

"Not yet."

The two of them continued browsing until James's phone dinged. He pulled it out and showed the message

to Mattias. Apparently Pierre had been successful.
James sent a reply, put his phone away, and returned
to the desk, reaching into his inner pocket and pulling
out his badge. "I'm Detective James Levinson, working with the sheriff's department, and we believe that
this ring may be stolen property. I'd like to see the records of its purchase, and you're going to need to put
it aside. We're arranging for the victim to identify the
item." James pulled his phone out again. "Is there an
inscription?"

The saleslady had gone white. She turned the ring
over. "My darling Rachel."

James nodded. "That matches the victim's
description."

"I'll need to call the store owner."

James nodded, and she went into the back. He
smiled at Mattias as she made her call.

Then she returned, took the ring from the case, and
placed it in the back room. "Mr. Anderson asked me to
show you all the records." She brought out a sheet of
paper with an inventory listing and the information on
the seller. "Mr. Anderson bought the items, but I did
the paperwork for him. They had a driver's license, and
that's where I took the information from."

"Thank you. Can you make me a copy of this?"

"Of course." She went in the back once again and
returned with a copy of the entire sheet. "Do you think
all of this is stolen?"

"It's likely, I'm afraid. Gather it all together, and
we'll see if we can try to find the owners." At least
James had a name and address, though ten to one he was
willing to bet that all of the information they had was
likely fake. "Can you please give me your name?" He
pulled out a notebook and took down her information,

all the business information, and then got down to what he hoped might lead to something. "Can you describe the person who sold you the items?"

"I really can't. I only saw her for a few minutes. Mr. Anderson dealt directly with her, and he said he's on his way. It will take him a few minutes to get here." She busied herself pulling items off sale, and James grew angrier by the second. Here was yet another victim of these people. They not only stole from the people whose homes they broke into, but now this business owner was out what he paid as well. Everyone was a loser in this game.

"Thank you." He stepped away and let her go about her depressing business. Mattias joined him. "I bet a lot of this is from our victims."

"And the rest from people we don't know about yet," Mattias said quietly, his eyes much softer than James had seen before. "This is why I quit the business. There were way too many victims." He turned away and found a bronze in the corner on a pedestal that captured his imagination. James figured he'd give him the time to collect himself. It was a harsh awakening to realize that your behavior only hurt others. It was possible for people to rationalize just about anything, but it got harder when the victims weren't nameless and faceless, but real people looking back at you.

"Did you see anything else that might have been on our list of stolen items?"

Mattias shook his head. "I didn't see anything, but then again, I don't have it memorized."

"May I help you?" a man asked as he entered. He was probably in his fifties, with graying hair, very distinguished.

"We're sorry to inform you that it appears you have purchased merchandise that was stolen," James said. "We have someone coming down to identify a ring, but she told us of the inscription, which matches. And it seems the other items you bought at the same time were likely stolen as well."

"I'm Harold Anderson, and I own the shop. I'll do what I can to help you." He scratched his head as he sighed. He looked as though he were in pain. This had to hurt. "I remember her pretty well."

"So it was a woman?" he asked for clarity.

He nodded. "She seemed the nervous type, about thirty, maybe a little over five feet. Nice-looking, bright eyes, spoke softly and was dressed nicely, but looked like she'd been struggling. Her clothes matched the story she'd told me about her and her mother needing to sell the items."

"She had a driver's license," the lady behind the counter interjected.

"I did everything right," Harold said, much more softly.

"I understand. We believe these are professionals, and if it's any consolation, we believe that these people are very good at fooling others. You were taken in by them, and I'm sorry about that." James explained to Harold what he needed to do.

They talked until a tall, older lady came in asking for James. She introduced herself as Rachel Himes. He explained who he was and showed her the ring. She identified it easily, along with three other pieces, which he tagged as evidence.

"Can I take them now?" Mrs. Himes asked.

"I'm afraid not. We will need them for evidence, but you will get them back." It was the best he could tell her. The wheels of justice sometimes ground to a near halt. But they had recovered her property, and hopefully once they got the thieves, things would move fast enough that the case could be resolved relatively quickly.

James took down all pertinent information from everyone, and once he had everything, did one last check of the store with the victim to ensure nothing else was there. Mattias hung back, watching and staying out of the way.

"That really sucked," Mattias said once the woman was out of earshot, when he and James had a moment. "I didn't realize it would take so long for her to get her property back. I probably should have, with the number of departments that I've worked with."

James shrugged. He wished he could make things move faster. These people had been traumatized by someone breaking into their homes and stealing their things, and now, when some of what they had lost was recovered, they had to wait to get it back.

"Is there anything else?" Harold asked in a defeated tone. There seemed to be plenty of that going around. Not that James could blame any of them.

"Not at the moment. Thank you." James took the evidence with him, giving Mr. Anderson a receipt for the items they believed had been stolen, and one to Mrs. Himes, who seemed somewhat relieved, even if she couldn't take her property right now.

"Do you think you'll be able to recover the other items that were taken?" she asked, holding her purse with both hands as though she expected someone to try to take it at any minute.

"We're trying very hard, ma'am," Mattias said, and damned if the way he said it didn't seem to make some of the tension leave her. "The detective and I are doing our level best to see that everyone gets back what was taken from them." He stepped forward. "Would you like me to see you to your car?"

She nodded, and James thanked Harold for his help and cooperation. Then they left the store, with Mattias seeing Mrs. Himes to her car before returning to theirs and getting inside.

"I hate this part of my job."

"What?" James asked, a snarky comment on the tip of his tongue.

"Seeing what I did to people in order to make a living," Mattias answered softly. "I used to be the one who hurt people like that and then dumped stolen merchandise on unsuspecting merchants. That's why I said what I did yesterday. There is no such thing as a victimless crime. Instead, the victims and people who get hurt only pile up." He turned toward the store. "How much longer do you think Harold Anderson is going to be able to stay in business if he purchases items that he can't ultimately sell because they're stolen?"

James nodded. "And as far as I can see, he did everything the way it should have been done." He stopped, got out of the car, and hurried back into the shop. "I'm sorry to bother you, but did you happen to make a copy of the driver's license?"

Harold shook his head. "That isn't our policy, but it will be from now on."

"Okay. Thank you." James returned to the car and pulled away from the curb. He should have thought to ask about the license earlier, but this case was getting to him more than he wanted to admit to anyone. "Let's try the next store."

Mattias simply nodded, and they drove in silence toward Mechanicsburg.

THE JEWELRY store on a major corner was quiet when they walked in. Mattias looked from case to case and asked if they had any estate jewelry.

"That's in the back showroom," the young, bright-eyed saleslady answered, and led them through a door to a smaller room. She flipped on the lights, and two cases of jewelry lit up, as did ceiling lighting for dozens of art deco statues. "The owner has been collecting the artworks for years. Some of it is for sale, but this area is for our estate jewelry. Is there anything you're looking for?"

James wasn't going to prevaricate. "I'm Detective James Levinson, and this is my associate, Mattias Dumont. We're working with the sheriff's department on a string of burglaries in the county."

She nodded. "Yes. We heard of those, but I doubt we have any of the items you're looking for."

James nodded. "I hope that's the case. Are there items you've purchased recently?" he asked, and she became nervous, wringing her hands, which made James wonder if something was going on.

"I'll call Mr. Powers. He lives next door. Excuse me." She returned to the main store, and James let Mattias look around while he assessed the exits and how quickly they could get out of here if anything unexpected happened.

"Detective, Marvin Powers." Mr. Powers smiled as he came in and shook James's hand. "Maryann was telling me what you need, and I'll do what I can to help. I've only purchased three items recently. Most of what gets brought in isn't up to our standards." He went be-hind the cases, unlocked a file, and pulled out three sheaves of paper. James was happy to see that he'd made copies of the identification used during the purchase. Mr. Powers set them on the counter and opened the cases to pull out two small rings and a brooch.

Mattias excused himself, leaving the room while James reviewed the paperwork. He returned with his computer and opened the lid. "There are no brooches reported."

James set the corresponding documentation aside and then checked the other pages, showing the picture to Mattias. "She matches the description, doesn't she?" James asked.

Mattias nodded. "Perfectly," he agreed, and James looked over the paperwork. The description on the form, especially the inscription mentioned, matched one of the items.

"Where is this ring?" James looked through what had been presented.

"It sold the day after I received it. I had a customer from out of town. He said he was visiting family. He saw the ring and bought it right away. I have the purchase information right here." Mr. Powers's hand shook a little as he handed over the copy of the receipt. "He paid cash, and as you can see, he was from out of state. It was nice and of good quality, but the stone was glass and not sapphire, so the price of the ring was based mostly on the setting."

James made notes and then glanced at Mattias, who finished looking through the other cases and re-joined him.

"I wish I could help you, but there isn't anything else I can do." Mr. Powers made a copy of the sales slip and handed it to him. "As you can see, he gave me a name and nothing else. It was a cash sale."

"I understand."

"I'm willing to give the people it was taken from the money from the sale. I know it won't replace what they lost, but it's something… I guess."

"I'll let them know. Thank you for offering." The law would probably require him to do that, but it was kind of him to offer. "I'll need a copy of your intake form as well."

"Of course." Mr. Powers made copies as James asked additional questions, taking down details for his report, and then they got ready to leave. James thanked him again and went through to the other room.

"I'm sorry. I must have dropped my phone in there." Mattias made a show of patting his pockets and hurried back inside. He came out a minute later with his phone, and Mr. Powers closed the door.

Mattias left the shop, and James followed him to the car. "What was all that about? You never took your phone out." He glared at Mattias, his suspicions rising.

"I wanted to take a quick peek without them there," Mattias said. "I only had a minute."

"Did you find anything?"

Mattias growled. "I don't know. Like I said, I only had a few seconds, but there are some things behind the counter that I'd really like to take a look at. I did manage to get the top off one, and it may have been the locket I was telling you about. I'm not sure because I had to leave." He shook his head. "That was a man all too eager to help so we'd get the hell out of his store and stop looking around."

"He was?" James asked, not having gotten that vibe from him at all. "Look, you're here to help, but you can't be breaking into things and sneaking around. That isn't going to work."

Mattias turned in the seat to face him. "But what if it was the locket? Then we'd actually have a way to trace him to the thefts. And he lied to you. Doesn't that piss you off?"

"Yeah, it would if I thought he was lying, which I don't. If he were regularly dealing in stolen goods, he'd have better paperwork and wouldn't have just had the merchandise on display. That would just make things too easy." And this case was going to be anything but easy. "At least we got a picture of one of the thieves. The name and address are probably fake, but I'd like to show this picture to Mr. Anderson to see if this is the person who sold him the jewelry." This could be their first real break in the case. Though facial recognition was nowhere near as easy as it was on television.

"Makes sense to me," Mattias agreed.

James sent a copy to Pierre and then contacted the other shopkeeper, hurrying back to the store, where he did confirm that she was the person he'd met.

HE AND Mattias got something for lunch and were headed back to the station when his phone rang. James glanced at the screen and groaned.

"An ex-boyfriend you don't want to talk to?" Mattias teased, and James stifled a growl.

"No. It's my mother," James explained, and hit the button to answer the call. "Hey, Mom." James tried to sound enthused, but a stab of apprehension ran through him. She usually called when she needed something or someone was in trouble.

"Hi, Jimmy. You're alive and not lying in a ditch somewhere, dead and bleeding."

Mattias put his hand over his mouth.

"I'm fine. Just really busy. And just so you know, I'm in the car and I'm not alone. I have an associate here with me." James hoped that would help his mother practice some decorum. "But when I saw you calling, I wanted to make sure you were okay."

"We're fine. Your father is on another of his business trips, and I hope he'll get home soon." She sounded down, but not depressed.

"Where is he?" James's suspicions rose and flew outside the car like a damned flag.

"Down south somewhere. I think Tampa. He said he'd be gone a few weeks and then that will be it. He's retiring." She made the announcement as though it were monumental. James had been hearing that for the last ten years.

"You know he can't stay away," James said, trying not to grit his teeth. His only saving grace was that his parents lived in West Virginia, but the entire situation was almost more than he could bear.

"But his hands ache now in the winter, and he's only happy when it's hot. So he says that after he's done this time, he and I will move to someplace warmer." She seemed happy, and James replayed the conversation quickly in his head to make sure it sounded completely innocent. Of course it did. But as soon as James glanced at Mattias, he knew the two of them weren't fooling him.

"That sounds like a great plan, Mom. I need to get back to work, but I'll call you later, I promise." James hung up, and Mattias stared at him, hard, his arms crossed over his chest.

"Well, that was the most strained and incredibly coded conversation." Mattias shifted his gaze slightly. "What is it your father does?"

James groaned and ran his hands down over his face. He swallowed hard as they approached the station, and sped up, deciding that work and being busy were his only chances at avoiding the questions he didn't want to answer.

He called Pierre, telling him they were nearly back, then parked the car, got out, and climbed the steps to the station, feeling Mattias's steely gaze behind him. But a conversation about his mother and father was the last thing he wanted to have at the moment.

CHAPTER 5

MATTIAS CHECKED with his hotel, but they weren't answering, and Clay told him that the power was still being restored. Apparently there were issues beyond the line being cut. Power was expected to return later today, but Mattias still didn't have a hotel. James was as jumpy as a long-tailed cat in a room full of rocking chairs, and had been for most of the day. The others wondered why out loud, and Mattias stayed out of it and as far away from him as he could.

James claimed he had a ton of paperwork to finish, but Mattias understood classic avoidance when he saw it. He, Clay, and Pierre spent much of the late afternoon throwing around ideas on patterns and trying to make sense of the data they had, but didn't get very far. At the end of their shifts, Clay and Pierre headed home, and Mattias waited for James, trying not to think about spending the night on Old Stinky in the changing room, but figuring something like that was definitely in the cards with the way James had been acting.

"Are you ready to go?" James asked. "We got a report of another burglary. This one is just outside Carlisle. I called Clay and Pierre, and they're already en route." He was halfway out the door before finishing his thought. Mattias packed up his computer, slid it into his bag, and followed at a half jog to catch up.

The drive seemed like minutes, and then Mattias was out of the car, staying away from the heart of the action because the house was a crime scene and he didn't need to make James any more uptight.

"I came home from work and the back door was partially open," a woman in her early thirties said as she stood on her front lawn. Mattias could imagine what they took: nothing bulky or big, but everything of compact value. And he was right, as she went on to describe the ordeal, her hands shaking.

James led her back into the house, and Mattias followed behind, his hands in his pockets, looking through the immaculate home as he went. They went to the living room and had her sit on the sofa. Mattias stood nearby, wanting to listen but also needing to stay out of the way.

"I'm sorry for your loss. I know this is hard, but can you tell me anything else? Let's start with what's missing."

She pulled a tissue out of the container on the side table. "My mother's and grandmother's rings. They weren't valuable, but it's all I have of theirs." She pressed the Kleenex to her eyes. "My father had a pinkie ring. He was a first responder after 9-11. He drove to the city and worked for months on the pile that was left. He died a year later of an infection that ate him alive. That ring was so precious to me." She buried her face in the tissue, and James let her sob.

"Is anyone else here with you?" Mattias asked.

She shook her head, and Mattias came around and sat next to her. She held his hand as he sat still. "Is this okay? I mean, police officers...." Her makeup ran down her cheeks, and Mattias grabbed another tissue from a nearby box.

"I'm not a police officer, and you can hold my hand all you want." Mattias couldn't turn away from someone who was hurting this much. "Just take your time and tell the detective what you can, when you can." He took a deep breath, met James's gaze, and let her compose herself.

"I'm sorry," she said after a minute, and dabbed her face. "I'm trying to think of all that's gone, but I'm finding it hard."

"Did you have any insurance records or pictures?" Mattias asked.

She swallowed and nodded. "I have them on a drive in the lockbox in the basement. At least I think I do, unless they took that too." She stood, and Mattias let James take her downstairs. They returned with a box that seemed intact, and she sat down on the sofa again. "John, my ex-husband, always picked on me because I had one of these. He thought I was being paranoid, but it's where I keep the important papers and things like that." She unlocked it and pulled out a zip drive. "They're pictures I took on the table. There's nothing fancy, but it should have images of everything." She seemed to have regained some composure.

"Let me get my computer, and we can go through them all and you can tell us what's missing." Mattias went back to the car, got his bag, and brought it in, then unloaded and booted up his computer before putting in the drive. There were five hundred images on the drive. Apparently she wasn't kidding when she said there were pictures of everything. And they were in no particular order, so they went through all of them, with her shaking her head most of the time and then stopping them at an item that was gone.

It took a while, but the expected pattern emerged. Twenty or so items were taken, jewelry, silver, a few small bronze pieces that were probably the most valuable of everything. James took down the information, and Mattias copied the drive to his computer, then removed it and handed the original back to her.

Mattias wanted out. The walls were closing in, and he needed a few minutes to himself. Not that he figured he was going to get it, but her raw emotion had gotten to him in a big way, and Mattias needed a chance to process it. "Is there anything else for now?"

James shook his head. "We've worked the scene and have everything I think we can get. The guys are running down possible witnesses, and you look dead on your feet." He led the way to the car and unlocked the doors.

Mattias got in and leaned back in the seat, closing his eyes. He was too tired to argue, and his mind swam with fatigue. He expected James to take him back to the station, but they ended up at James's house. "Hopefully the power will be on later tonight and I can go back to my hotel and get out of your hair."

James humphed but didn't actually say anything.

Mattias followed him inside and collapsed into one of the living room chairs. "How can you do this every day? You see people hurt one another and have to talk to people like her all the time. Life threw her a shit sandwich, and you have to try to help make it right again."

"Very interesting metaphor," James quipped as he sat down as well and put his feet up. "I'll get some dinner together soon. Right now, I don't think I can eat after that." He leaned forward, catching Mattias's gaze.

"No way."

"Yeah. I have sandwich stuff for dinner, but I think you just killed that idea." James smiled. Mattias liked it when he did that. He got the idea that smiling and generally being happy wasn't something James did a lot of.

"Why don't I make dinner?" Mattias offered. "I'm a pretty good cook, and if you show me what you have, I can put something together."

James rolled his eyes. "You sure about that? There isn't a lot in the house. I eat out a lot and spend a great deal of time alone." He pushed himself up as well. "Cooking for one is hell."

"Tell me about it," Mattias added. "I like cooking, but most of the time I either make too much and end up eating the same damned thing for a week, or I get one of those meals-for-one things in the store and heat it up." He went into the kitchen, opened cupboards, and pulled out some things. "There's pasta. That's always a good starting point." He continued looking before opening the freezer and then the refrigerator. "You weren't kidding." Mattias found some cheese, and there was milk. He dug in the freezer and pulled out a bag of green stuff.

"Mom made that for me. It's her basil mixture."

Mattias grinned. "Pesto. Oh, there is a God." He got to work and soon had water on to boil for the pasta, mixed up a little pesto cream sauce, and found the things for a salad. "It looks like you had a feast in there that you didn't know about." He pulled out a chair for James. "While I do this, you can tell me about that stuff with your mom."

"I was hoping you'd let that go." James sounded almost as thrilled to talk about that as he would to be getting a root canal. "I don't suppose that's possible." The chair scraped on the floor while Mattias cut up a tomato.

"You don't have to." Mattias figured giving him an out was the nicer thing to do.

"I never talk about my family with anyone… ever." James leaned on the table, and Mattias started slicing a cucumber that had seen better days but still had good parts. "Mom and Dad…." James sighed. "My father is a jewel thief. It's what he's done for as long as I can remember. He cases homes and spends months planning his heists." He patted the table with his hand.

"Okay…."

"I never saw my dad do anything, and he's never put me or my mom in a compromising position. His work was his work, and he didn't bring it home. I found out by chance once when I came across a diamond the size of your eye in his car. It was an accident, and I never went near anything he drove or carried again."

Mattias put the salad together and set the bowl on the table. "So you lived the life too?"

"Yeah. Dad got caught when I was fourteen, and went to prison for a year. That was the hardest time of my life. I was in school, and all the other kids knew where my dad was. I saw those looks and endured their taunts until Dad got out, and we moved as soon as his probation was over. It was a new school, and Dad said we had a chance at a new life. But he was back at it soon enough and has been ever since." James shook his head. "I vowed to have nothing to do with that and wanted to be a cop so I could help the kind of people my dad hurt."

Mattias nodded. "I understand. I really do." He patted James on the shoulder. "Do you see them often?"

"No. They live in West Virginia, and that conversation with my mom was telling me that Dad is in Florida pulling some job. I don't want to know what it is, but it kills me. It's the eternal moral dilemma. Part of me says to turn him in and let the chips fall where they may. But he's my dad, so I turn a blind eye. Mom knows, and she pretty much does the same. It's how they've lived for decades. Spending your life in denial and self-justification isn't the way I want to live. I need my life to be clean, and I need to feel good about what I'm doing."

Shit, that was quite a revelation. "I really do understand that." Mattias put the pasta in the water to cook, stirred it, and then sat down next to James. "I suppose it's my own confession time."

James stood and got a bottle of wine out of one of the lower cupboards. "If we're going to share stories like these, then I think we could both use a little fortification." He poured two glasses, and Mattias finished making dinner before rejoining James at the table with a dish of pasta and a story.

"I had a shitty childhood. Well, not all of it, just most of it. My parents are out there somewhere, I like to think. But I never knew my dad, and my mom… she didn't want me. When I was about five, she left me with my grandma and grandpa. Those were the happy years. They took me places, and I went to school. All the stuff normal kids did." Mattias shook his head and dished up some of the rigatoni and salad. "I suppose that was the really good part. I lived with them for four years until they died in a car accident." Mattias swallowed around the lump in his throat and coughed on the bite he'd taken. "Look, this is a crappy story, and you don't need to hear this stuff."

James took a large drink of his wine and then refilled his glass, then added some more to Mattias's afterward. "There's no law that says you have to tell me anything." James's eyes twinkled. "You have the right to remain silent."

Mattias groaned at the bad joke but smiled anyway. "Cute."

"I thought so." James wagged his eyebrows.

Mattias found himself laughing. He took another bite, this one going down without incident. "Anyway." He might as well get this over with. "They died when I was nine, and I ended up in the foster care system, shuffled from place to place, trying to make myself invisible. And that I was good at. I stayed places for longer because I never made trouble. But at sixteen, one of the foster fathers decided I was pretty… and I was out of there. From then on, I took care of myself, and I learned how to steal. That was how I survived. I took what I needed, and then more and more as I figured things out. I broke into my first house when I was seventeen, and stole stuff I could pawn at the drop of a hat. I survived and got a fleabag apartment that I paid cash for by the week. I continued working, cased houses." He set his fork down. "I spent my money on decent clothes, good haircuts, and plenty of soap and water to stay clean. Nobody gave me a second thought when I cased their houses because I looked like I belonged there."

"So you didn't have a mentor like in the movies?" James asked.

"The movies are just fantasy. You know that life is a lot grittier than that, and more basic. I was feeding and housing myself. I had some money put away, and I stayed under the radar. I almost got caught a few times, but I needed to live, so I continued stealing… for nearly ten years." Mattias paused and took a drink of the wine. It bit his throat as it went down, but he needed that.

"What changed?" James asked. "People don't make huge life shifts without something to pull them out of themselves. I'd have thought that my dad being in jail would do it for him, but it only made him more determined to continue the life he'd had before."

Mattias took a few bites, trying to get his thoughts together. "I came face-to-face with what I was doing. Like today with that lady." He paused and tried to talk, but the words wouldn't come right away. "The place I lived was pretty basic, and the neighborhood wasn't very good. Mrs. Wellerman lived on the first floor. She had only Social Security and mostly stayed inside her apartment. One morning I heard her crying. Someone had broken in, while she was there, and taken what little she had." Mattias set down his fork and lowered his gaze. "Her husband had been gone ten years, and she had almost nothing left. Just her wedding ring, which the thief stole right off her finger. They also took her husband's ring and a few other things. All she had left of a forty-year marriage was gone… *poof.* Just the fuck like that." Mattias felt the anger and shame from that day well inside him again. "She was helpless, and I wanted to do something." He sighed. "I contacted the people I dealt with, and sure enough, the asshole had sold them for a few dollars. I found them in the shop, bought them back, and broke into her apartment while she was sleeping and put them on her kitchen table. That was the last crime I committed. I couldn't do it after that." He blew air out of his mouth. "I tried more than once, but every time, I saw Mrs. Wellerman and how torn up she was over those little items that I bought back for a few hundred dollars. To the thief, to me, they had just been things to turn into cash. But to her it was a hold on the past—a better, happier time—and I was taking that away from people." He drained the last of his wine and was grateful when James poured some more.

"A thief with a conscience," James said without heat or sarcasm, which was good, because Mattias was pretty sure he wasn't going to be able to take it right now.

"No. I think I grew a heart, like the Grinch." He ate a few more bites and sat back, his appetite gone. "It took me some time to start the business I have now, but it's legitimate, and I haven't taken a thing from anyone, except the fees that I earn, in eight years. I can't replace the things I stole, because they're gone, but I can try to make up for what I did by stopping others." He blinked and leaned over the table. "That's why we're going to find, catch, and nail these bastards to the wall."

James raised his glass, and Mattias did the same, lightly clinking them together. "To the past and putting it behind us."

"Amen." Mattias emptied the glass down his throat. He needed something to drink and thought of asking for something stronger than wine, but that wasn't a good idea. He knew that when he thought he needed a drink, it was probably best to refrain. "I never talk about that. It's over and in the past." He sighed and brought over his bowl of salad to eat because he needed something to cover his discomfort. "I try to forget it, if I'm honest."

"But it doesn't work," James said, and Mattias nodded. "You can't forget part of who you are. You can alter the person you want to be, but part of who you are…?" He tilted his eyebrows. "I've spent a lot of my teen years and adulthood trying to get away from what my father is. I can't change him."

"Yeah, but you know what your dad does, yet you don't turn him in." Mattias leaned forward. "That has to ring a lot of moral bells. You're a police officer."

James nodded. "Yes, and you're a thief. You told a room full of police officers that. It's part of who you are." He got up, went into the dining room, and returned with a box. He set it on the table and opened it. "This was a gift from my mom and dad when I bought the house."

Mattias lifted out one of the forks and turned it over. "Beautiful, Gorham silver, sterling, over a hundred years old. High quality and desirable even today when the market for silver flatware is running low." He set the fork back.

"See, you appraised it without even thinking. And I never use it and keep it in the cupboard in the dining room because I have no idea where it came from. I have researched robbery reports in case it was reported stolen, but I can't look everywhere in the country. Someday if I find out it does belong to someone else, I'll return it to them." James closed the lid. "I can't enjoy something that beautiful because I don't know where it came from." He set the box aside, and Mattias's gaze followed it for a second, but then he pulled it away. "I haven't been able to enjoy anything that came from my parents because of its origins. Even if my mom gave me a receipt, I'd know where the money she got to buy it came from." James sighed. "It really sucks, and taints every interaction I have with them. So yeah, the bells go off all the damned time, and I don't know what to do about it."

"When was the last time you saw them?" Mattias asked, feeling some of James's pain. For a good share of his life, he had wished he had real parents, someone to love him and take him out of the foster care system. He used to dream about it all the time. Mattias knew his mother was out there somewhere… and for a while, he used to wonder if she would come to find him. But that was a long time ago.

"I saw them at the holidays. I went down there to visit for a few days. It was difficult for me." James leaned back in the chair. "I wonder about everything they have and what my dad is doing all the time. After three days, I had to come home just to stop the worrying. Dad doesn't think about any of it, but I can't get away from the hypocrisy, and I know it's of my own making. They don't feel any of it." He shook his head, and Mattias saw the conflict raging in James's eyes. It had probably been there for years.

"At least you have them," Mattias said. "They're there, and they support you and love you, even if you are on two sides of a moral dilemma."

"Yes, they do." James finished his wine and tossed the bottle into the recycling. "Do you want some more?"

"I'd better not." If Mattias drank more, he'd end up even more maudlin than he felt at the moment.

"Do you know your mother's name?" James asked. "I could try to find her. There are databases that I can use. If you know her full name and place of birth, things like that, I could try to see if she's alive and where she lives."

Mattias shook his head. If she'd been out of his life for this long, he didn't need her now. "It's probably not a good idea." Part of him was afraid, and always had been, that she'd reject him yet again. It was better for him not to know and to just go on with his life than to try to find her. Mattias stood and started to clear the table. Some activity to keep his head somewhat clear.

James put his hand on Mattias's arm, and he jumped, nearly dropping the dishes. He'd been so deep in his own thoughts that he hadn't heard him get up. "It's okay. I know this is a tough idea. I was only offering to help."

"I know. And if you had asked me at a different time in my life, I probably would have jumped at the chance to try to find her. But there's no use now. She has her life, wherever that is, and I have mine." It would have been nice if she'd come back after Nana and Poppy had been killed. That was when he'd needed his parents the most. Not only had he lost the two people he loved most in the world, but he'd found himself with no home and no one to care for him.

"Did your grandparents leave you anything?"

Mattias shrugged. "My mother was still in their will. So everything was a mess, and I have no idea what happened to any of it. The state probably took everything to pay for my care." He sat back and half closed his eyes, watching James. "You know, some more wine or something isn't such a bad idea." Maybe these memories coming to the fore, the ones he thought he'd pushed back and locked away, just needed to be forgotten forever... or at least for now.

"I have some really good vodka," James offered. He got the bottle out of one of the cupboards and set it on the table with a container of ice and some grapefruit juice. Then he took care of the dishes while Mattias mixed up some greyhounds, and they moved to the living room and more comfortable chairs. "Let's talk about something more interesting."

Mattias snickered. "Like surgery without anesthetic?"

"Or maybe the last time I had a colonoscopy." James shuddered.

Mattias narrowed his eyes, wondering what was going on there. That was something people older than James generally had. Did he have health issues?

"Maybe we could talk about plans for peace in the Middle East. That could take all night," Mattias offered. James raised his glass, and Mattias followed, drinking a healthy—or actually, an unhealthy—amount.

James emptied his glass and set it aside. Then he laid his head back on the chair and closed his eyes. "This is such a bad idea," he whispered.

Mattias wondered what he was referring to. Sitting here drinking, yeah, he could probably agree, but Mattias got the idea that wasn't what James was talking about, especially when his incredible eyes slid open and the temperature in the room rose by ten degrees in as many seconds. Mattias shivered—not from cold, but from the intensity of being held in the tractor beam that was the line between James's eyes and his. He couldn't look away, no matter how many times he told himself he should, or that this was indeed a bad idea. Mattias's heart thumped in his chest loudly enough that he was sure it could be heard in Pittsburgh. Still, he remained motionless, afraid to move, yet almost as afraid not to.

James slowly, almost in slow motion, got to his feet and crossed the distance between them. Mattias blinked and pressed back into the chair as James placed his hands on the upholstered arms, the frame creaking slightly with the additional weight. He blinked, James blinked, but their gazes never faltered. James licked his lips, and Mattias did the same, as though he were under his spell. Then James drew closer; finally, their lips touched.

Mattias was prepared for a gentle kiss, but what he got was a ravishing of lips and tongue, sending his spirit soaring and his libido through the roof. Breathing was secondary. This had to continue, because stopping and those lips pulling away would be like taking something precious and long sought and throwing it away.

It did end. Mattias panted and thought of pulling James back in for another when James turned away and, without a word, climbed the stairs.

CHAPTER 6

JAMES HAD to get out. The few brain cells that weren't steeped in alcohol screamed at him to stop. The rest of his brain yelled that he was being fucking stupid and to get back down there, kiss the ever-loving fuck out of Mattias, and maybe sling his skinny ass over his shoulder, carry him upstairs…. James leaned against the wall as his head spun from the thoughts running around in rapid little circles like a hamster on a damned wheel. The alcohol was supposed to stop all that shit, but instead it was only getting worse.

He breathed deeply, only to get a huge whiff of his own toxic breath in return, and decided the best thing was to go to bed and try to sleep all of this shit off. But one thing was for sure—he might have had enough to drink to muddle his brain, but he hadn't had enough to make the erection that had been throbbing for most of the evening go down.

James made it to the bathroom and splashed water on his face, then quickly brushed his teeth to rid his mouth of the residual alcohol taste. Footsteps on the stairs told him that Mattias was on his way up. He hurried and zipped across the hall to his room, closing the door on temptation before he could second-guess

himself. This was the right thing to do. He had lived
his entire life with a thief in the family—not that his father hadn't provided for them and done his best for the
family.... He hadn't treated them badly. But James had
long ago decided to dedicate himself to being on what
he saw as the right side of the law, and getting involved
with Mattias was flirting with that line a lot more than
he could allow himself.

James got undressed and climbed into bed, turning out the bedside lamp. The room was bathed in
blessed darkness, but it did nothing at all to calm the
whirling desire that ran through him. He closed his
eyes, and instantly Mattias was there, slipping under
the sheets next to him. James rolled over, his imagination—probably fueled by the alcohol—taking off on
a flight of fantasy he wasn't at all sure he should be
taking, but after denying himself the reality, this was
his only consolation.

His HEAD thumped and felt swollen. James slowly
got up and padded to the bathroom for some pain re-
liever. He took the pills, drank an entire glass of water,
and then opened the door, turned toward his room, and
bumped into Mattias, who was coming the other way.
James grabbed him to keep from knocking him over,
and they ended up chest to chest, skin touching, sending heat instantly racing through him, and his addled
brain into overdrive.

Mattias held him in return, one of his hands gripping James's upper arm and the other cradling him
around the waist. Under different circumstances, they
might have begun to dance, but Mattias closed the
distance between them and kissed him firmly. James

stepped away, the wall pressing to his back, and Mattias came right along with him, pushing hard. Maybe dancing wasn't such a bad idea, though getting horizontal was sounding like a better and better idea all the time. Thankfully, Mattias seemed to have the same notion, and guided him out of the hall into the master bedroom. James slid back on his own bed, with Mattias joining him, his weight pressing James deliciously against his own soft sheets. Why hadn't he done this earlier? The answer eluded him as Mattias again took possession of his lips.

Damn, he had known Mattias was hot, but not energetic and as radiant as a live wire. James held him tightly as Mattias writhed on top of him, gliding his hips back and forth, sliding their cloth-covered erections alongside each other. James closed his eyes, whimpering slightly while trying the hell not to. He hated that his mind was still clouded and wished he'd been sharp enough to be able to remember every second of this. Sure, it might be a mistake, but if it was, it was certainly one he wanted to be able to recall.

"Jesus," Mattias whispered into the darkness between them.

James stiffened. "What?"

Mattias ran his hands up James's chest, pressing some of his weight against him. "You're made of rocks. Hard, warm, smooth, sexy rocks." Mattias petted him, and James chuckled from deep in his throat. James was ready to give Mattias something that was rock-hard and was about to tell him so when Mattias cut off the words with another kiss and slid his hands down along James's side, hooking his boxers as he went and tugging them down his hips. They were gone soon enough, and Mattias's went along

with them. Naked, skin to skin, heat building between them, Mattias writhed slowly, undulating in a
sort of dance that held James spellbound. It had been
longer than he wanted to admit since he'd been with
anyone in an intimate way.

"What's got you sunk into your head?" Mattias
asked, tugging James a little out of himself.

"Nothing," he answered quickly—too quickly—
sliding his hands down Mattias's back to cup his incredible ass in an attempt to cover up.

"Uh-huh." Mattias hummed and leaned closer, his
lips near James's ear. "I know when a man is conflicted
and fighting with himself, and I can pretty well guess
what it's about with you." He tugged James's earlobe
with his lips, sucking on it, crossing James's eyes because it felt so damned good. "I told you I don't steal
anymore, and I certainly don't take what isn't freely
given." Mattias stopped.

James tightened his hold on Mattias's butt, pulling
their hips together. He wanted this. His mind snapped
into gear, and he realized just how much he longed for
the intimacy. James rolled Mattias on the bed, pressing him into the mattress. He kissed Mattias forcefully,
pouring how much he wanted and how freely he could
give into each and every yearnful kiss and flick of his
tongue. Mattias held on to him, giving himself right
back and clenching on to him just as hard as James was
holding Mattias.

Maybe, just maybe, this was something they both
needed, and maybe if they held on and saw this through,
whatever it was, James could find something he was
missing—that they both were missing. That thought
flashed through his head and was then obliterated by

a blaze of passion that burned away everything else, leaving him bare and wanting.

JAMES WOKE hours later, as light was just starting to slip in through the windows. He wasn't alone. Mattias lay next to him on the bed—well, half over him was a better description—and he radiated heat in all directions. James actually thought of trying to slip out of the bed and going downstairs, anywhere other than here where he was going to have to look Mattias in the eyes and attempt to make some sort of sense of what had happened. James had thought he'd done the right thing and tried to stay away. Still, he wasn't a dick, and sneaking away was a pure A1 dick move, so he lay still and closed his eyes, listening to Mattias breathe.

When he came to once again, he was alone, the bedding still warm but the covers empty. It seemed Mattias wasn't above sneaking out of bed, and that sent a jab of anger and relief running through James. At least he now had an excuse to ignore what had happened. Then Mattias filled the doorway.

"I put a little cream in your coffee, the way I saw you took it at the station," Mattias said as he came in, boxers hanging on his hips. He sat on the edge of the bed and handed James the mug.

James sipped from the nectar of life and sighed. Mattias leaned against the headboard, stretching out next to him, legs crossed at the ankles as though he were completely comfortable. James did his best to ignore Mattias and concentrate on his coffee, but it was impossible.

"Ummm."

Mattias turned slowly to watch him. "I take it you don't want to talk about last night." The levity in Mattias's voice got right under James's skin. "You know not talking about things doesn't make them go away, and it isn't going to change the fact that we slept together... for at least part of the night." He turned and smiled, but James wasn't sure what that meant. "I know you were still a little in the bottle last night." Mattias slipped off the bed as he finished the last of his coffee.

"Okay. I probably was." James could admit that, and at least that gave him an excuse.

Mattias set the mug on the nightstand and leaned close to him. "Judging by last night, I can't wait to see what you're like completely sober. I bet you're one hell of a fantastic ride." He picked up his mug and left the room.

James didn't watch his ass swing slightly from side to side as he went. At least that's what he told himself.

MATTIAS CHECKED his phone from the passenger seat. "Apparently they have the power fully restored now and I can return to my hotel."

James nodded, figuring that was probably a pretty good idea and an easy way to remove temptation. "You should call to make sure everything is okay." He breathed a sigh of relief as he continued the country drive toward the sheriff's office. He yawned and listened as Mattias made his call. It was fairly clear within the first few seconds that things were not going well.

"You what...?" Mattias asked and shook his head before pulling the phone away. "They had a water leak in the fire suppression system, and the first floor of the hotel flooded. I'm going to have to try to find another place to stay." He returned to the hotel operator, telling her to cancel everything for his stay and that he would find somewhere else. Then he hung up and began making other calls.

"Just stop. You can stay at the house. It's stupid for you to try to find another place." What was really stupid was that James was making this offer in the first place. Yet… part of him was intrigued, and the more he thought about what Mattias had said, the more he wondered exactly what had happened last night. James definitely needed to remember to drink less.

"Are you sure?" Mattias asked. "You've been weird all morning… quiet… even solicitous. That's sort of freaking me out." He set his phone on his lap. "I know you were weirded out after what happened, but it isn't going to affect how we work together. You and I will be professional, and then tonight, after work, we'll see what happens." The heated, almost prophetic expression reminded James of the cat about to eat the canary, knowing it had caught it and the delight was waiting to be savored.

Thank God, they approached the station. James pulled into the lot and parked next to Mattias's car. Tonight they could each take their cars to the house—that way Mattias would be free to come and go on his own.

He shut off the engine and was about to get out when Pierre bounded down the steps and to the car. "There's a robbery in progress on Market Street in Mechanicsburg. The local police are responding, but they called because it could be related to our case. Clay is heading right over there."

James closed the car door again and pulled out, taking off away from town as quickly as he could. He was really getting tired of being two steps behind these people, and if they could catch them in the act, even some of them, they could have the chance to solve this case. Solly would be thrilled, Mattias would be out of his house and out of his life, and the conflict waging inside James would resolve itself.

He drove like a bat out of hell, full sirens and flashing lights. People pulled over on the country roads, and he whipped through traffic signals as he came into town. James made the turns at speed and arrived at the address he'd been given, where police cars already filled the street. He pulled to a stop and got out, looking for the officer in charge. It didn't take long to find her coming out of the house, a stormy expression on her face.

"James," she said, coming to a stop.

"Hey, Marie, what did you find?" James asked, exchanging a quick glance with Mattias.

She shook her head. "Sorry. It seems someone jumped the gun on this one. A neighbor kid, thinking the house was empty, broke in and tried to steal the television and computers. The kid thought he could make a few bucks and get back at the homeowner for calling the police on his party last Saturday." She rolled her eyes. "We have him in custody and are going to transport him. I'm sorry that you got called out here."

"Well, shit." James looked for the others on the team and issued them instructions to go back to the station. After he was done, he turned to tell Mattias they were leaving, but he was nowhere to be found. James groaned and wandered among the cars. He found

Mattias standing at the door to the back seat of the police cruiser.

"What were you thinking?" Mattias was asking through a slightly cracked back window. "This isn't going to go away, and now this little incident is going to follow you for the rest of your life." As James approached, Mattias grew quiet. "Please. I made my living as a thief for almost ten years. I know what the fuck I'm talking about. You sell your damned soul to the devil, hurting others, to get what you want. It doesn't work out in the end." The boy seemed to be listening, so James took a step back, giving Mattias some room. "Who cares if you don't get caught? It still eats at you from the inside." Mattias shook his head. "You'll find out, believe me." James backed away from the car, and Mattias saw him and came over. "Are we done?" He didn't even wait for an answer before heading back to James's car and getting in.

James slipped into the driver's seat and started the engine. This had been a waste of time from a case perspective, but the effect on Mattias was unexpected, and James once again didn't know quite what to make of him. Part of James wanted to be able to take Mattias at face value… and another part warred with his former profession. James put the car in gear, but his foot clamped down on the brake to stop the car from moving. *Former profession.* James realized that, in his head, he'd acknowledged Mattias had changed his life. Being a thief was what Mattias had done, but it wasn't who he was now. Maybe James needed to give him the benefit of the doubt. He shook his head to clear it and pulled slowly away from the crime scene, heading back.

"What the fuck was that kid thinking?" Mattias asked when they were about halfway back, his hands clenched to fists. "He was stupid beyond belief and has no idea how much he has changed his life for the worse. Sure, if this is a first offense, then he might not go to jail, but his record is going to stay with him for the rest of his life in one way or another. And he stole a lot more than just a television and a few things."

James nodded. "I know. That family just had their security and peace of mind ripped away from them. They won't go on vacation without worrying about what's happening back home. They might install a security system or have neighbors watch the house for them, but their lives have been changed, all because some kid wanted to get some extra money." He tried not to think about how many people his father had stolen their security from.

"Yeah… well, we never think much beyond what it is that we want." Mattias turned to him as James pulled to a stop. "It's all about ourselves. We need to survive, or we need to buy that next fix, or we want that video game system… or whatever, and someone else's things are right there. All we have to do is take them, get out and away, and that's pretty much the end of it. I was never caught, and frankly I never thought I would be. No one does. We all think we'll get away with it forever." Mattias slumped in the seat.

"What are you worrying about?" James asked. "My dad?" It was a guess, but an educated one, given their conversation from the night before. Mattias nodded and said nothing more. For some reason James felt a little put out. "Why?" he pressed.

"Because of what he's doing to you," Mattias finally answered. "I know how that whole situation is wearing on you and leaving your loyalties divided. I've been there. My career divided my own until I came face-to-face with a victim." He shook his head.

"I always wonder if my dad ever actually saw the people he was hurting. Or if he did and just didn't care." James gripped the wheel tighter. This was uncharted territory for him. He rarely talked about shit like this with anyone. Not that he didn't need to or hadn't felt as though he wanted to talk, but he'd never found anyone he thought could possibly understand. "I keep wondering what I should do."

Mattias nodded. "There's nothing you can do. You love your dad and don't want to hurt him or your mom. Turning in your dad will do both those things. But not saying something will continue to pull on your soul until it either rips or you let it go. And neither of those things is preferable." He grew quiet. "My only advice is to talk to your father and tell him he either has to quit or you will turn him in. Give your dad the chance to do the right thing." Mattias patted his arm. "You owe it to your dad to give him the chance, and you owe it to yourself to take some sort of action to relieve this conflict."

Just hearing Mattias say those words seemed to change something inside him. He had come up with the same course of action some time ago, and if truth be told, he'd been afraid to have the conversation. "What if my father decides to do neither, and he and Mom simply move on and I lose them both forever?"

"You mean, like go on the run… from you?" Mattias asked and shook his head. "Is that really practical… at their age? They could try to hide, but they can't run from both you and the law."

"True, but in a way, I'm asking them to choose between the life they've both had and me… and how I feel." And what if they didn't choose him? That was always the difficult question. It was coming out all over again, only this time it was much more substantive. James wasn't just asking them to accept who he was— he was asking them to change part of who they were. "Can they change? Is it possible?"

Mattias shrugged. "You won't know until you talk to them."

James couldn't argue with Mattias's logic.

He pulled into the station and parked in the same spot he'd used earlier. Mattias got out, and they walked side by side into the station, where they were met by the sheriff.

"Have you seen this?" Solly asked, handing James a printout of an internet page once they got to the squad room. "It seems my opponent, Skip Parker, is spouting that we aren't able to solve this spate of robberies, and that if he were in office, he would. Of course, that's bullshit, but it makes for great campaigning, and people are getting scared as reports build up day after day." He dropped the pages into the trash. "Get this case solved, and do it fast before this entire situation blows up and becomes so big that—" Solly swallowed.

"We'll do our best," Clay said forcefully. Solly had the loyalty and dedication of the men under him. "We'll get the entire department to help if we have to." He and Pierre turned and strode toward the workroom to get started, and after Solly left, James and Mattias did the same. There had to be nuggets of information in what they already had. They just needed to find them.

"WE'RE GETTING nowhere looking at the same information again and again," Clay said with frustration

as he scraped his chair on the floor. He got to his feet
and began pacing.

"I agree," Mattias said. "What we need is more information, but we don't have any at the moment. We
need to find some." He smiled, and James's belly fluttered a little. Mattias closed the report he'd been re-
viewing yet again. "I'm not saying that these reports
aren't complete, but...." He stood as well, sighed, and
left the room, the door closing with a thud behind him.

James wasn't sure what was going on, and he got
up to go, but Pierre shook his head. "I think he may
need a few minutes."

"Why?" James asked.

Pierre seemed surprised. "We're used to this. It's
what we deal with every day. He wants to help you
solve this case... badly. I think he's taking this person-
ally, given his background and the changes the guy has
made in his life. And he isn't used to our usual level of
frustration." He raised his eyebrows.

"What do you think he's doing?" James looked at
the closed door.

Pierre and Clay glanced at each other and then
back to him. "I think he's probably calling some old
friends to see if anyone has heard anything. Maybe
contacts that are still active," Pierre said.

James shook his head and strode toward the door.
"This isn't some damned television show. We have to
do things correctly." Besides, after the last few days,
James was beginning to understand just how much
something like that could cost Mattias. Yeah, the people he might know... maybe they could help him, but
at what cost? What pound of flesh would they try to
extract from him? James was well aware that no one
did something for nothing. Not in those circles.

"Yes. But we need information, and Mattias just might be able to procure some." Pierre turned away and returned to one of the laptops that sat on the table.

James hurried out through the station to the front door. He found Mattias in the parking area, out near the road, talking on his phone. James watched as Mattias ended the call and put the phone in his pocket. He sighed before turning, and James knew the instant he saw him, his eyes brightening for a second and then growing darker.

"I have an appointment this evening… and I have to go alone."

"Over my dead body," James growled. "What do you think you're playing at? This is a sheriff's investigation."

"We need information, and a friend of a friend might be able to point us in the right direction." Mattias's expression changed. "I can't involve you in this."

"You already have. If you agreed to some sort of meeting…." He held Mattias's gaze, watching the uncertainty grow. "Then you know what price they're going to extract, and I won't allow it."

"You don't get to tell me what I can and can't do. This is my decision, and I can make it perfectly well on my own." Mattias's lips formed into a line.

"Yes, you can, and I can make my own decisions as well. And if you think you're going to any meeting that involves this case alone… you're sadly mistaken. Now came back inside, and we'll figure out how to make sure you're properly… protected." He waited for Mattias and followed him inside. "Where is this meeting?"

Mattias paused and turned, his hand on the door. "At the shop where we're having you measured for your tuxedo. I didn't tell my contact who you were, but I figured it would be best if someone were nearby in case of trouble." His eyes glimmered with mischief.

"You manipulative bastard," James said without heat.

"At least I know you care about my virtue." Mattias wagged his eyebrows, and James rolled his eyes. He should have known when Mattias gave up too quickly.

"What I care about is that no one puts themselves in danger or does anything to impugn the reputation of this investigation or the department. I need my professionalism intact once this case is over."

Mattias didn't bat an eyelash. "Bullshit. You want this case solved just as much as I do. Besides, the police use informants and get information from a number of sources to solve cases."

"Don't be flippant," James said, placing his hand on Mattias's shoulder. "You know damned well that no one does anything for free."

Mattias sighed, the amusement slipping from his eyes. "I'm well aware of what might be required. But we need some information that we don't seem to be able to get any other way. When the time comes, I'll be prepared to pay whatever it is I need to." He pulled open the door and went inside.

James followed, anger building. "I will not have—"

Mattias whirled around. "Just let go of this head of steam. I can handle whatever comes up. This isn't my first time around the block. This meeting may yield exactly nothing. Or we could get lucky and get the piece of information we need to finally get a break. Just relax." He sighed. "You'll be with me. How much trouble can I possibly get into?" The mischief had definitely returned, and James wondered what he was allowing himself to get into.

THE TUXEDO shop looked like any other shop in the strip mall. Mannequins stood in the windows, dressed better than James ever had. "Are you sure about this?"

"We need to get you measured anyway. I already have the tickets for the charity event, and you need to be dressed properly." Mattias motioned toward the door. "If you want to wait here until after I've met with my contact, that's perfectly fine." He strode toward the shop door, and James huffed, following him inside. This seemed like a strange place for a meeting.

Mattias went right inside and spoke with the older gentleman behind the counter. "Great."

The man took James over, measured him for a shirt, and tried a couple of jackets on him. "Do you need shoes?"

"I have black dress shoes." James tried to pay attention, but also kept an eye on Mattias as he wandered the store. It was a bit like watching a tennis match. No one else came into the store, and James wondered if the guy who at that moment was running a tape up his inseam was the person they were supposed to meet.

"What sort of tuxedo did you have in mind?" the man asked.

"A standard black jacket and pants, but I think a deep red tie will add a hint of color," Mattias answered. "We could go with a gray vest...." He looked over the display of various tie and vest combinations. "I think not. Simple is better with these kinds of things."

"Very good. Let me get your information, and I can have what you need here tomorrow."

James followed him to the desk and provided the information requested. When he turned around, Mattias was nowhere to be seen.

"Where did my friend go?" James asked, stepping away to peer around one of the display walls. He hadn't heard the door open or close, and it had one of those beepers on it, so Mattias had to be here somewhere. James finished paying, and Mattias joined him once again, standing at the counter. Once James had his receipt, they left the shop. "Where did you go?"

"Nowhere," Mattias answered.

"Was he your contact?" James asked.

"No." Mattias smiled as a lady, probably approaching sixty, exited the shop. "Carrie," Mattias said, hugging her.

"It's been too long." She turned to James. "Is he cool?"

Mattias nodded.

"Okay. I thought you were out of the business, so I was surprised to get your call. You need a job or something?" She took Mattias's arm as they walked down the sidewalk in front of the shopping center, with James following behind.

"I'm out of the business, and I intend to stay out. You know I've been working with the police." James had to give Mattias credit for being honest.

"Is he a cop?"

"Yeah. But he's okay. James is only interested in the same thing I am—who is behind these robberies." Mattias stopped their walking. "These guys are hurting people, real people like you and Bill. We need to put an end to it."

She patted Mattias's cheek. "You were always too kindhearted for the business." She glanced back at James, distrust clear in her pinched expression.

"No. I think the business got a hell of a lot nastier than it needed to." Mattias turned to her. "Do you know who is behind these robberies?" Mattias pressed, but Carrie shook her head.

"No one I know or ever had dealings with. Work it out, though. They seem to strike where they want." She leaned close and spoke something directly into Mattias's ear.

Mattias smiled and then kissed her cheek before turning back to James. "Please go to the car. I'll meet you there in a few minutes." He turned without looking back and led Carrie away, their heads close together.

James wondered what the hell those two were up to and considered breaking them up. Hell, if Carrie knew information that could help them, then there was likely something in her past that James could use against her. His cop instincts came forward, along with a touch of righteous indignation. But he held himself back, going to the car and standing next to it as Mattias led Carrie around in front of the TJ Maxx at the far side of the parking lot. She got into her car and drove off. Then Mattias returned and got in the car.

"What did she tell you?" James demanded. "And who is she?"

"I introduced her to you. I know that's not her real name, but it's the only one that I will tell you. And she wasn't going to let you see her car so you could trace her license plate. Carrie is an old bird, and she's survived as long as she has by being careful."

"You don't trust me?" James asked, wondering why that notion hurt a little.

Mattias rolled his eyes. "Why should I trust you when you're so Trusty McTrustful yourself? It goes both ways, you know. I can say that she's heard of our people and says they are from out of town. Apparently they came to her, trying to sell some things, but she wasn't buying."

"Where did she say they were from?" James asked, not starting the car yet.

"She wasn't sure. It was hard for her to place, but she thought it might have been somewhere farther south." James got the feeling that Mattias wasn't telling him everything. "The woman who matched the description from the auction house tried to sell her the locket. She had a feeling it was hot and declined, but Carrie did say the woman had someone else out in the car, and she thought she saw a kid as well."

"A family of thieves?" James asked with a sigh.

"I don't know, and neither did she."

"Why is she helping us?" James asked and turned on the engine, the air-conditioning cooling the interior of the car.

"Because people like this... they hurt everyone. Carrie knows what's happening, but she isn't a bad person. She doesn't buy stolen goods, but often they are offered to her. I'm sure you can understand that. If there are thieves operating in the area, then everyone— antiques, pawn shops, anyone that does resale of any kind—has to be careful, and it hurts their ability to do business." Mattias seemed to relax, but James wasn't letting this go just yet.

"What else did she tell you?"

Mattias pursed his lips. "You don't get to ask those questions. She and I have known each other for some time." He turned to James, and the glare lowered the temperature in the car by the second. "If you must know, she was the one who helped me build a new life. Carrie used to have an antique store in Philadelphia. She ran it for years, and then she was robbed. They took everything she had, cleaned her out. After that, she didn't have a business any longer or any way to support herself. Everything she'd worked for all those years… *poof…* gone, like that. The police found nothing."

"And did you try to help her?" James asked.

Mattias nodded. "Let's leave it at that, okay? I owe her quite a bit for helping me put my life on a different track. She helped hold a mirror up in front of my face. And she always had her ears to what was happening. Her son had moved here after college, so when she was able to retire, she came here and opened a small shop in Carlisle to supplement her Social Security." He shook his head. "I meant it when I said that thieves steal people's lives. I've seen it." He grew quiet.

"Okay." James turned in the seat. "But was she able to help point you anywhere?"

Mattias sighed. "She didn't know a great deal other than what I already told you. This isn't like television, where someone always knows what's going on. Carrie did confirm that the people we're looking for have children. Remember how we found the toy?" Mattias paused and his eyes widened. "James, can you take us back to the station? I need to get to the reports and the computer."

"You have an idea?" James asked as he backed out of the parking space and drove as fast as he dared toward the station. "What are you thinking?" he asked once he was on the freeway.

"What if the kids aren't just the kids? What if they're the thieves? What if this whole thing is some kind of family affair? Houses aren't easy to break into."

James wanted to hit himself on the side of the head. "You mean like Fagin in *Oliver Twist*?"

Mattias nodded. "I've known people to use kids to get into homes. They can crawl through much smaller spaces, through tiny windows into basements, through doggie doors. People don't think of things like that. And then once inside, the kids unlock the doors and the adults take over." Mattias snapped his fingers. "Who would think of young kids, or even look twice at them?"

"Jesus...." James drove faster and got them to the station. Mattias was quiet, and it was dark when they arrived. Mattias followed James inside and went right to the spreadsheet they had created.

"Yes...," Mattias said. "Look at the times of all the robberies. All of our witnesses put the robberies either first thing in the morning or in the evening. Now, there are some that aren't specific, but they could all have happened at those times." Mattias looked at him, and James shrugged, not making the connection. "They're happening before or after school."

"Holy shit...," James breathed.

"Yeah. It's frightening." Mattias leaned back.

James got on the phone, called the sheriff, and explained they had a theory. Solly came right down and closed the door.

"What have you got?" he demanded.

James explained what they thought. "It's got merit. And we found a new witness who said the woman passing off the stolen goods had a southern accent. Maybe we can contact the schools and see if any kids match the description." His heart raced with the challenge of the chase.

"You're sure about this?" Solly asked.

"I don't think we can be sure of anything," Mattias said. "But I think this has the potential to be a good lead. The times all match, and we did find a child's toy at the scene of one of the robberies, as well as information that there was another person and a child when someone tried to sell some of the stolen property." Mattias explained what was being sold and how distinctive it was. "This is worth taking a chance on."

Solly nodded. "Talk to the various principals, but to no one else at the moment. I don't need every teacher in the county coming after me." He wiped his forehead. "Follow this lead, but tread a little lightly."

James agreed, and after Solly left, he sat down to draw up a list of schools and people they needed to speak with. It was quite a list, and James divided it among other officers on the team.

"What about me?"

"I think the school contacts are best left to us. I know you want to help, but since you aren't a parent and don't have specific business with the schools, they aren't going to let you in. Security is tight." James leaned closer. "Do you want your name logged in as a school visitor?" He wasn't being a dick, just practical. "Do you want anyone looking into your background that closely if something should happen?" James didn't think Mattias would, and after he shook his head, he finished up the task. "We might as well go on home for the evening. We need to get here early so everyone can start making calls and setting up appointments." Maybe he could get a few additional deputies to fan out and ask questions. This was going to be a bigger task than he'd originally thought, but it was a lead. And with the right questions, they might be able to make some progress. Kids talk to one another and to adults. They say things they don't mean to. It would only take one suspicious teacher or principal to put them on the right track, and James needed to find them if they were out there. "Are you ready to go?"

Mattias nodded and gathered his things. "I'll meet you at your house." He smirked, and James wondered just what he had in mind when they got there.

CHAPTER 7

MATTIAS DIDN'T like lying to James. Well, he hadn't been lying exactly, but he'd left out a number of things from his conversation with Carrie, including asking her a favor. He'd also bypassed the fact that Carrie's real business was information. She was expert at procuring it and at selling it. That was what she'd always done and why Mattias had called her. The rest of what he'd said had been true. He'd really felt bad asking, but James was very conflicted regarding his dad, so Mattias had inquired about any information regarding James's father that she could dig up to see just how bad things were.

"Do you think he's involved in what you two are working on?" Carrie had asked.

"No. I don't think so. But he's up to something, and James is worried about it. I get the feeling it's that one last big score, and you know how things like that usually turn out." Mattias had seen it more than once. Overreach and desperation to set themselves up for retirement often led people to do things they normally wouldn't and to take unnecessary risks. Mattias didn't think James would be able to take his father getting caught and ending up in jail once again.

She'd clicked her tongue lightly. "I see." Carrie patted his cheek once again. "Of course I'll see what I can find. The usual price?"

"I'll have the chocolates sent over." She loved Lindt truffles, and her family seemed to think them a wasteful indulgence, so Mattias sent them to her. He leaned down and gave her a kiss on the cheek before letting his gaze wander across the parking lot to where James waited, leaning against the car.

"He has great energy," Carrie said. "If I were younger...."

Mattias smiled. "It's a good thing you aren't—otherwise I wouldn't stand a chance."

She snickered as she opened her car door. "Somehow I don't think that man is ever going to be interested in me, but he can't take his eyes off you." She smiled once again.

"He doesn't trust me," Mattias said dismissively.

Carrie nodded. "Or maybe it's himself he doesn't trust." She slowly climbed into the old car and closed the door. Mattias backed out of the way and watched as Carrie drove off, before heading over to where James waited.

"ARE YOU still with me?" James asked, pulling Mattias out of his daze. "I'll meet you at the house."

Mattias blinked as he looked around, realizing he'd sort of zoned out. "Yes, I'll meet you there." He thought of just telling James what he'd asked, but decided not to. It was a long shot that Carrie would be able to come up with anything about James's dad anyway. Mattias left the station right behind James.

He got in the car and followed James to Mechanicsburg, a drive that was becoming quite familiar now. He parked and paused at the front door, not sure if he should knock or not. James opened the door before he could knock, and Mattias went inside.

"I thought we could order some takeout," James said. "It's been a long day, and I'm tired." He led Mattias through to the kitchen and handed him a menu.

"No problem." Mattias sank into one of the kitchen chairs, looked at the menu, and chose the sweet-and-sour chicken. Then, while James placed the orders, he went upstairs and changed into some more comfortable clothes. He hoped James didn't mind. And judging by the way James stared when he returned in a pair of shorts and a T-shirt, James didn't mind at all. Maybe Carrie *was* right.

"Ummm… do you want something to drink? I have soda and sparkling water. After last night, I figured it's best if we stick to soft drinks."

"Whatever you're having is fine." Mattias went to sit in the living room, waiting for James to return. But he seemed content to fuss in the kitchen, and when he did come in, he brought Mattias's drink and left again.

"I'm going to go get the food," James called in.

Mattias brought his drink into the kitchen once James was gone, and got out plates and silverware. It seemed so domestic. Mattias could get used to this kind of life. He'd been alone for a long time. Hell, in one way or another, he'd been on his own for much of his life. He hid behind a wall of snark and a disarming smile, but they were only defenses, and he was well aware of it.

James returned with two plastic bags, set them on the table, and went upstairs. Mattias got out the food, and when James came back down in a T-shirt and sweatpants, dinner was ready.

James sat down, dished up his food, and began to eat right away.

"You don't like to talk about things, do you?" Mattias asked after he swallowed.

"And you seem to want to talk about everything," James snarked in return, then sighed. "If you want to talk about last night, then talk." He rolled his eyes, and Mattias stifled a snort. Dang, he was cute when he got frustrated. James could take charge of a crime scene instantly, but when it came to the mention of things between them, he could only look at his plate, occasionally glancing up, probably to see if Mattias had melted into the floorboards.

"Why are you so repressed?" Mattias asked.

"I am not!" James protested more loudly than needed.

"Sure you aren't." Mattias leaned over the table. "We had sex last night. Hot, sizzling, groping, mind-blowing sex that rocked my world," he said breathily.

"We did all that?" James whispered, and Mattias chuckled.

"Well, you were an animal for about fifteen minutes, and then as soon as the deed was done, you fell asleep." Mattias rolled his eyes. He loved getting under James's skin.

James's cheeks reddened. "I don't remember anything, other than a few vague recollections."

"And you're acting this repressed?" Mattias teased. "You have nothing to be ashamed of... believe me." He smiled, hoping James would see the humor in the situation. "It happened, and you can ignore it if you like. But not talking about things isn't going to make them go away."

"And you want to talk about it?" James mumbled. Mattias took another bite and figured he could wait James out. Eventually he'd want to say his piece. "Dammit. Last night shouldn't have happened. You're staying here in my house, and we work together, and…." His thoughts fell off.

"You're really grasping at reasons." Mattias nodded. "That's fine. I can definitely take a hint. And I won't pressure you into anything. You can be sure that I'll be able to keep my hands off you if we happen to meet in the hallway during the night." He shook his head and did his best imitation of James, eating and growing silent.

"Jesus, you're snippy," James retorted. "I never said any of that. I just don't know how to talk about things like this."

"Haven't you had a relationship with anyone?" Mattias asked.

"I've had sex, if that's what you're asking. But no real relationships. I fell in love with this guy after I left the academy. He was really kind of sweet, but he began pressuring me to meet my parents and that I should meet his. I couldn't do that. How was I supposed to explain what my dad does and equate that to my job as a police officer? 'Oh, by the way, I'm a cop and my dad is a thief. Yes, it's weird, but my family is just that way. I ignore what he does, and he does the same for me.'" James's fork clanged on his plate. "It just wasn't going to work."

"Jesus," Mattias breathed. "Your father's profession affected you that much." He could see pretty clearly that James's dad had done more than steal jewels. He'd taken his own son's peace of mind along with everything else. "But you're safe with me. I know, and I don't look at you differently." He reached across the table to tap James's hand lightly. "You can talk about anything you want. It isn't going to shock me."

"Yeah… well. That's easier said than done."

"Okay. Then how about if I ask the questions. Did you like what happened last night?"

James seemed to think for a few seconds and then nodded. "Yeah."

"Do you want it to happen again?"

"Yeah. But it probably shouldn't. We work together, and things could get weird." James finished the last of his dinner and took his plate to the sink.

"Weirder than they are now?" Mattias pressed.

James set his dishes in the sink, turned around, and began laughing. Finally he saw the humor in the situation.

"See?"

"Sometimes you're a giant pain in the ass," James told him.

Mattias shrugged. "I've been told that before. But seriously, just sit down and tell me what's going on in your head. What is it you think you want?"

James pulled out the chair and sat down. "I don't know. That's the problem. Since you got here a few days ago and have been staying here, I've liked it. It's been nice having you here, and the house doesn't seem so empty."

"So this is a generic person staying here because you're lonely," Mattias said. He could live with that as long as it was honest.

"No. I've had people stay with me before, and I never wanted to take them to bed." James grew fidgety. "I find you attractive… like, you push all my buttons, okay?" He huffed and leaned forward, holding his head in his hands. "You're smart, funny, and you don't take any shit." He slowly raised his head so Mattias could see his eyes. "And you see through all my shit. No one has done that before. Not even my mom and dad ever seemed to see through to the real me."

"Okay. So why are you so scared of that?" Damn, Mattias sounded like a shrink, and he hated that. "Forget I asked that stupid question."

"Why?"

"Because being vulnerable is scary as shit. I know that. I don't go around sleeping with people, and I don't get close to people very easily. I had to learn to rely on myself, and others… well, they screwed me over—or they tried to. I could tell you stories, but maybe those are for another day." Mattias paused as James leaned forward. "Because they're not pretty, and you aren't going to like it, and, well, I want you to like me." There, he'd said it. Wanting someone's approval gave them power over you, and admitting it to them only added to that. "So I guess I get that you're scared, because I'm scared too. This seems like new territory for both of us."

James swallowed but didn't argue. Mattias didn't think James was the kind of guy to admit fear, and that was okay. Sometimes admitting you were afraid allowed the fear an entrance and the chance to take over. So many times, Mattias had survived difficult, nearly compromising situations by keeping a clear head and talking his way into an out. Fear was something that had to be managed; it could help keep you sharp and on your toes. It could also petrify you into inaction.

"Is that enough talking?" James asked.

Mattias laughed. He couldn't help it. "Yes. That's enough talking."

James turned away. "I hate talking."

"I think I got that." Mattias tried not to smirk, because James seemed dead serious. Their banter back and forth was cool, but with the stone-cold expression in James's eyes, something had definitely changed, and it concerned him.

James leaned over the table. "When I was a kid, my dad… he used to talk all the time. It was what he did, and whenever things didn't go his way, he talked and weaseled his way out of it worse than a crooked politician. It got so that I didn't listen to what he said, and then to what other people said. I tend to judge people by their actions."

"I see," Mattias said. He tended to do the same. He had spent years in a business where lies and fraud were normal and expected. Everyone had an agenda, and rarely was it fully understood. Cross the wrong person and you could end up with a knife in your back even as they smiled at you. "Playing things close to the vest is a good thing for a lot of situations, but I can't read your mind." Mattias took care of his dishes and threw away the containers. Being useful was the least he could do, given that James was letting him stay here with him. "Though I try to watch your expressions."

James's chair scraped on the floor as he pushed it back and turned it. "How so? I'm pretty good at schooling myself."

Mattias didn't want to start an argument, but this was too good to pass up. "Okay. Right now, you have your lips pursed slightly, so you're defensive and you think you can intimidate me. Why, I don't know, considering what happened the day we met. When you're happy, you have this smile that doesn't go to your eyes, but it makes a little line appear right here." He ran his finger over James's upper cheek. "And when you get excited, you practically bounce on your heels, which is what happened when we figured out that the kids might lead us to the thieves." Mattias leaned a little closer. "And when you get really excited, your eyes get wide and your mouth parts just a little, as though you're surprised that you could feel that damn good."

"Mattias…," James growled.

"You think that's going to work? You're two seconds from smiling because you're damned proud of yourself, and if I'm not mistaken, you're remembering a little more of last night than you admitted to." He loved this and the way the color rose into James's neck and cheeks. "Do you really want me to go on?"

James shook his head. "Am I really that much of an open book?"

"You mean to the guys?" Mattias placed his palms on James's shoulders. "No. They look at you as a colleague and nothing more. At first, I watched you because you fascinated me, and frankly I thought you might be a threat. Then you came to my rescue, and I thought that maybe there was a heart behind the badge." He ran his hands over James's shirt, tweaking his nipples when he encountered them. "Last night I found out about everything under this detective's suit and tie."

"You think so?" James placed his hands on top of Mattias's, their heat melding together.

Mattias held still, his fingers itching for more. "Yeah. I found a heart and someone who craves being touched but doesn't seem willing to admit it." He closed his arms around James, who eased up on his hands, still touching him but no longer trying to stop him.

"Mattias… that mouth…."

He chuckled. "What? I haven't even begun talking dirty yet." Still, he could almost feel James's heart beating under his hands, and the musky scent that wafted around him was more than enough to tell him just how much he was affecting James. He loved the fact that James shook a little bit and was doing his best to control himself. Mattias intended to stretch James's control to the breaking point and see just what the man had when he let go.

"This is you being clean?" James mumbled.

"I haven't said a single word that I wouldn't say to your mama. Sometimes the sexiest things are the ones that leave a lot to the imagination." Mattias leaned over, running his hands down James's belly and then back up when his hips started rolling. He really was getting to James, and he started to wonder how long it would be before James took over. The guy was way too alpha for words, and Mattias liked that. He also loved poking the bear to see how quickly he could get a rise, and it seemed he was getting one right now, if the tent in James's pants was any indication.

"Maybe, but I bet you'd still never talk to my mama the way you did."

Mattias groaned. "I wouldn't be talking to your mama or having the ideas I am with her either. So how about you and I go on upstairs and put these ideas into action?" He tugged James to his feet. "We can stand here and circle each other all night long…."

James got up, turned out the lights, and led Mattias through the house and up the stairs. "Go on into the bedroom. I want to check the doors downstairs so I don't have to get out of bed later." James pushed him back on the bed. "And dammit, be just like that when I come back." He sped away, thumping down the stairs as Mattias kicked off his shoes, listening as James hurried around below, thudding on the wood floors, before barreling back up the stairs.

"Is this what you wanted?" Mattias asked, lying on the bed, his head on a pillow, his gaze following James through the room as he paced like a caged cat. "You nervous?"

"Yeah…," James admitted, and Mattias sat up. "I know it's stupid, but…."

He took James's hand. "You have nothing to be nervous about. This is going to be good for both of us. That's what sex is. It should be fun, not a source of consternation." He tugged James toward the bed, then kissed him as he lured him closer. "We can take our time, and we don't have to be anywhere until tomorrow morning." God, he hoped that was true and that no phone calls came in to make him a liar.

"Let's hope," James whispered.

"Even cops have to have some time when they aren't working." Mattias tugged James down onto the bed. "Join me for a while, said the spider to the fly." He was feeling particularly happy at the moment.

"That is such a bad analogy," James countered, pressing Mattias back onto the pillows. "Besides, I'm the spider, just so you know." He bared his teeth for a second. "Don't forget that."

Mattias chuckled, running his fingers down James's cheek. "You really think so? I'm the one with the wiles to lure you up here." He knew it wasn't fair, but he didn't give James a chance to argue, kissing him instead, tugging him down on top of him.

"You and your filthy mind," James teased.

"A dirty mind is a terrible thing to waste," Mattias countered, tugging at James's shirt, getting it up and over his head. Now *that* was so much better. Mattias just needed to get his off. He groaned, because James was no help, running his hands around his middle as soon as he lifted his shirt. Mattias laughed as James tickled him with his lips while he was stuck in his shirt. It was hard to concentrate with James's lips and hands on his skin. It was decadent to be touched that way. Somehow he managed to get his shirt off. He dropped it on the floor and lay back down.

"You're like a cat, aren't you?" James whispered as Mattias put his hands under his head. "You'll soak in all the attention as though it's your due." James licked a nipple, and Mattias hissed softly, closing his eyes.

"It's nice to have someone pay attention once in a while." He ran his fingers through James's soft, dark hair. "You know what it feels like to have someone want you and see you." He guided James's lips to his. "It doesn't happen that often, and I keep expecting to wake up—that you and this is all a dream somehow."

"Why?"

"You like that question, don't you?" Mattias kissed him again. "Because maybe nothing good ever really happens."

James rolled his eyes. "Or maybe you need to shut up and let the good happen." He cocked his eyebrows, and Mattias figured that maybe he was right, so he put his lips to better use. And damn, James was an amazing kisser—he knew exactly what to do with his lips.

Mattias groaned as James found a spot at the base of his neck that sent a quiver racing through him. He stilled and clamped his eyes shut, afraid to move as James slid downward, fingertips and tongue blazing a trail down his quivering belly. God, he wanted this to last, but with the way James had him wound up, he wasn't sure if that was going to happen.

Breathing deeply, he fought the urge to wrestle control from James and just went with his brand of pleasure, which quickly turned out to push all of Mattias's buttons. And the amazing thing was that James hadn't actually touched him yet. Their pants were still on, though Mattias was already throbbing in his shorts, desperate for more. James knew the magic of touch and care, even if, as he said, his relationship experience was limited.

"Jimmy," Mattias whimpered, and James paused. Mattias opened his eyes to find a deep gaze meeting his. "Don't stop."

"What did you call me?" James growled.

"Jimmy," Mattias said, as though it were natural. He ran his hands down James's back and over his rock-hard ass, gripping the globes with his fingers. "Damn, you really *are* made of rocks."

"Just shut up and kiss me," James demanded.

Mattias was more than happy to oblige, slipping his hands inside James's sweats, his warm, smooth skin sliding under his hands. James quivered and deepened the kiss while Mattias did his best to slide the material downward past James's hips, shimmying out of his own pants and shorts.

The two of them did this weird, demented dance that eventually ended with the pants on the floor and the two of them naked, pressed to each other. This was heaven, their heat melding, James slowly caressing him, sliding downward, trailing a line of heat that intensified and built until James slipped his lips down Mattias's length, stealing his ability to talk—hell, to even think.

"Jimmy, if you keep that up, I'm…." He gripped the bedding as a wave of ecstatic pleasure washed over him. He clamped his eyes shut, afraid to tell James to stop, but if he didn't, it was going to be over way too soon, and Mattias wanted this to last.

James must have sensed what he wanted, and backed away, leaving Mattias breathless and hanging on the edge. "What do you want?" James asked, and Mattias blinked out of his pleasure daze. "What will make you happy?"

So few people had ever asked that question, and Mattias found himself at a loss. He swallowed and shrugged before he could think much about it.

James kissed him and then asked again.

"Just take your time," Mattias answered, his mind way too clouded for rational thought. He wound his arms around James's neck, drawing him even closer, kissing him harder, letting the passion overtake him once again. This was what he wanted so badly, and he hadn't even realized it until now.

"I can do that," James whispered, and proceeded to worship Mattias as though he were truly something special.

Time had no meaning as James engulfed his mind in waves of pleasure that ebbed back, only to rise higher the next time. Mattias held on to James, and the bedding, trying to ensure he didn't fly away and explode into pieces of searing ecstasy. He was determined not to beg, but as time passed and the need for release grew greater and more urgent, he found himself doing just that, only to have James hold him off even longer.

"Are you ready?" James asked from over him, arms on either side of Mattias, sheathed erection poised and ready to enter him. James was the king of foreplay, and damn it all, Mattias was so ready. He nodded, and James entered him slowly, filling him so completely, he clutched his arms, begging for more. James paused and then continued, purposely driving Mattias out of his mind. The stretch was divine, the heat that surrounded him, radiating off James's body, was heavenly. When James filled him completely, pressing him into the sheets, chest to chest, his hips rolling slowly enough that Mattias heaved for breath, pleasure morphed to ecstasy.

He placed his hands on James's hard chest, their gazes locking, and for a few seconds, James was completely open to him—the hurt, the pain, the joy, and the happiness all melding together in his deep brown eyes. There are depths to anyone, and Mattias figured that being able to see them was a rarity. He hadn't even known if James had meant to show him so much of himself, but it had been there, written in his eyes for just a few moments. Then it was gone, replaced with tenderness and care, but the glimpse into James's soul had passed... or had been replaced, because Mattias wasn't going to last much longer.

James was magical, and he seemed to be able to play Mattias like an instrument that had been out of tune for years and was suddenly producing the most profound music imaginable. He clung to James, moving with him, his head growing light until he couldn't take it anymore. James filled his senses, from the musky scent that permeated the room, to deep groans and the vision of taut muscle before him. All of it combined to the point where Mattias couldn't take it anymore. His pleasure centers pinged again and again, his body on overload. He closed his eyes and let go of the last of his control, tumbling into release with a cry that echoed in his ears as his entire body tingled in sheer amazement as he let it wash over him.

Mattias lay still, his body aching in all the right places. James gently wiped his skin with a warm cloth, and he sighed contentedly, sitting up slowly to kiss him.

"I'll be right back," James whispered, and left the room. He returned a few minutes later and slid into bed.

"James... I...."

James put a finger to his lips. "No more talking right now. I promise we can talk about anything you want to in the morning." They settled in bed, and James spooned to his back, holding him tightly. "For tonight, just let things be, and try to stop wondering, okay?"

Mattias hummed his agreement. He didn't have the energy to talk right now anyway. He was happy, and Mattias would leave it at that. The whys and where-fores could wait for now, and his normally churning head could settle into quiet.

But the damn thing refused to, and after a half hour, Mattias lay in bed, his head running through possible scenarios.

"You need to close your eyes and relax," James whispered.

"That's a stretch coming from you." James never seemed to relax. "I keep thinking about these thieves and them using kids. It's got my mind racing in circles." He rolled over. "What I keep coming back to is why the thieves would put their kids in school. Why not blow into town, use them, and then leave again?

If I were going to do something like that, it's what I'd do. Keep everyone out of the public eye as much as I could."

"But you know how things are," James said. "They have to live somewhere, and if the kids aren't in school, neighbors will call Child Protective Services. It's how things work today." James tugged him closer. "Regardless, we have to follow every lead—it's part of the job." James kissed his shoulder. "So is getting some rest so I don't fall asleep behind the wheel tomorrow." He stroked Mattias's shoulder, and Mattias closed his eyes, trying to sleep.

CHAPTER 8

FIVE SCHOOLS and he was getting nowhere. James had talked to the others, and they'd reported the same thing. They were running out of possibilities. He had one more on his portion of the list, but Clay and Pierre were already heading back to the station. This was turning out to be a waste of time. Maybe Mattias was right and James was barking up the wrong tree. Still, he had one school to go.

He pulled into the Riverside Elementary parking lot and exited the car. James got out his badge, went to the front door, and rang the bell for entrance, looking up at the camera. It probably would have been easier to call, but he needed to impress how important this was and it was easier to put him off on the phone.

A woman came out of the office, the hallways filling with children flowing around her. "May I help you?" she asked from the other side of the door.

James showed his badge, and she let him in. "I need to speak to Principal Miller, please," James said. "Are you her assistant?"

"Yes. Gloria Malton." She smiled as the last of the kids passed by her. "Recess. Let the kids run off some of that energy." She opened the office door and led him inside.

A striking woman came out of the other office. "What can I do for you, officer…?"

"Detective Levinson, but please call me James."

"Kim Miller," she said, and they shook hands. She motioned to her office. "I hope none of my kids are in trouble."

He loved how she said "her kids," like she cared for each one. "Nothing like that." He took the offered seat. "Please stay as well," he told Gloria. "Look, I'm sure you've heard about the rash of robberies that have been taking place."

"Yes, of course," Kim said. "But what does that have to do with us?"

"One of the people involved has been selling the goods, and they've been seen with a child." He sighed. "We're checking with all the schools to ask if they could please keep an eye out and let us know if they hear or see anything. The woman they were with had a southern-type accent, and we suspect that they might have arrived in the area a few months ago…."

Both Kim and Gloria shared a look and then turned back to him.

"You know something."

Kim took the lead. "Yes. We had a couple of families move into the area, and they enrolled four children soon after the start of the school year. Classes had started just a few weeks ago." She seemed reluctant, and James couldn't blame her. "I have no idea if these families have anything to do with what you're looking for or not, and I can't allow you to speak with the children without their parents present."

James understood that, and he saw the problem. "I don't expect you to break any rules. However, if you could, check with their teachers to see if the children talk about anything unusual. I'm afraid it's possible that the children are being used in the thefts."

Both of them paled.

"How did you deduce that?" Kim asked.

"A number of things, including the fact that all the thefts are outside school hours." He leaned forward. "I'm running down any and all leads. As I said, I don't want you to break any rules, but if one of your teachers or either of you should hear anything, I'd appreciate it if you'd give us a call. We believe that these children are being used by their parents or guardians, and I want to stop the thefts and to help these children. They deserve a better environment to grow up in." He tried not to think of his own home life and how his father's profession had affected him, but it was damned near impossible.

"All right. I'll check with the teachers and inquire with my staff. If I hear anything, I will pass it along, as long as you promise to put the welfare of my children above everything else."

Dang, James wished he had had this lady when he was in school. She really seemed to care about the children. "Of course...." He began to stand, but she wasn't done.

"Do you know what this sort of thing can do to a child?" Kim pressed.

"Yes, ma'am. I am well aware of the fear and worry that a child can have. I also know what it's like to have parents who keep secrets and have lives that aren't necessarily conducive for raising children." He stood and extended his hand to shake with both of them. "I appreciate any help you can give me." He waited for Gloria to escort him down halls that were now quiet, and out of the building, then returned to his car and drove out of town to the station.

"How did it go?" Mattias asked when he entered their team room.

"I think I might have had some luck at the last school. It seemed like the principal had some idea of some possible kids, but she isn't going to just let us talk to them."

"Why not?" Solly asked as he followed him inside.

James turned to the sheriff. "Because we don't have any proof of what we're thinking. I can't blame them for not wanting to tell us what they suspect right away." James met Solly's hard gaze. "She's protecting her kids, which is what she should be doing."

"Do you think she'll call you?" he asked.

"If she finds out anything… yes." James was sure of that. The look on Kim's face had more than told him that if she came up with anything, she'd let him know. But that was turning into a big *if*. There were no guarantees that their hunch was correct, and hers was the only school that hadn't looked at him like he was completely crazy.

"Then what's next?" Solly asked.

"James and I have a charity function tonight, and home tours tomorrow. It seems these are two events that our thieves might use to try to check out people who might have something worth stealing."

"I contacted the historical society, and Mattias and I are 'volunteering.' The head of the tour knows who we are, but no one else does. I'm going to be working the ticket booth so I can size up everyone who buys a ticket. Mattias will be in one of the most lavishly decorated houses on the tour. From what I've been able to gather, the owners are going all-out and need docents because the ones they arranged for couldn't make it. If the thieves are going to case any house, it will be that one."

"And this charity event?" Solly asked.

"Plenty of people wearing their best jewelry and finery. It would be easy enough to check people out and either follow them home or simply engage them directly in conversation," Mattias explained. "It isn't hard to get people to open up, especially at an event like this where they are out and about to be seen and to have a good time. People are hoping to network and talk. It's a thieves' paradise, and all they need to do is buy a ticket." Mattias smiled, but the sheriff didn't.

"Where did the cost of the tickets come from?"

"I arranged for them," Mattias explained. "We also got some proper clothes so James and I will look the part. The whole idea is to mingle and keep our eyes open."

Solly nodded. "And what are you looking for?"

James opened his mouth, but Mattias beat him to it. "He and I will know it when we see it. People always work the room in fairly predictable patterns, going from group to group, introducing themselves, that sort of thing. Thieves are looking for something different from anyone else." Mattias pushed back his chair. "They may work the room, but they are not going to want to make an impression. They'll be there and yet try to not stand out."

"Sheriff," James interrupted. "Mattias and I are going on our own time, and the department isn't paying for the tickets. But if we see anything, we may need backup."

"I see." Solly didn't sound particularly convinced. "Of course we'll have someone available if you need it." He looked around the room. "Are you getting anywhere else?" He seemed nervous and set the local paper on the table. To Solly's credit, he didn't rant and rave about the headline, but the words were there in black and white. The lead story was the robberies in the county, and James had no doubt that Parker had a quote in it about the current sheriff. Hell, it wouldn't surprise him if Parker had somehow arranged for the story. But if James wanted Solly elected to the position he definitely deserved and had worked hard for, then James needed to do his job and get this case solved. He and Mattias had been brought in to specifically get that job done, and so far they hadn't succeeded in bringing the case to closure. That needed to happen—and fast. A success in the case would cut Parker off at the knees and give Solly a chance to show real success.

James wished he could say they were making great progress, but things were slowing down and leads were becoming harder and harder to find. "We're not going to stop, and they'll make a mistake or show themselves. When they do, we'll have them."

"Let's hope so." The sheriff left the room, and James shared a look with the other three.

"I don't know him very well, but I don't think that's quite his normal self," Mattias said.

Pierre and Clay both shook their heads. "Sheriff Briggs is the best," Pierre said. "He gave Clay and me a leg up when we needed it."

"Yeah, he was like a mentor, and I don't want to work for Parker…. No way in hell. We got rid of a political incompetent not too long ago. We don't need another one."

"Then let's solve this case."

James's phone pinged, and he checked it. "We need to go. There's been another robbery." He made a call and listened to the dispatcher, who gave him the address. "Thanks...." He ended the call. "This time someone was hurt. Apparently they came home while our thieves were inside." James was already halfway out the door before the others snapped into action. It looked like it was going to be a long afternoon.

HE CHECKED his watch for the fourth time. "I need to talk to him before you transport," James told the EMT again. This time they opened the back door of the ambulance, and James climbed inside. Mattias stood on the ground while the EMT prepared the victim to be taken to the hospital. "I'm sorry this happened, Mr. Gunther. Can you tell us anything about what you saw?"

He nodded, his eyes drooping. "Yeah. It was a man and a woman. The man hit me while the woman took my wife's jewelry box." He lifted his hand without the IV to his eyes. "They were all I had of her." He wiped his eyes and laid his gray head back down. "It was a man and a woman. I didn't see them very clearly, but I think there was a kid somewhere. I heard his voice, I think." He rubbed his eyes, and James sighed. He wasn't going to get anything more from him at the moment.

"You get better, and we're going to do our best to get your things back." He turned toward Mattias, who had an expression of incredible determination on his face.

"Thank you," Mr. Gunther said as James carefully climbed out of the ambulance. "I think they had a car. It was green. They parked it out in front of my house."

"Thank you for your help." James stepped away and made notes as the EMTs closed the ambulance doors.

"He didn't tell us anything we didn't already know. Other than helping to confirm that they are using kids… or at least have them along on their robberies," Mattias said. "We need to stop these people. They've hurt someone now, and they're either going to escalate, which is bad, or they're going to realize the heat is on and get the hell out of Dodge."

James was afraid of that. Solly's opposition was already trying to use the robberies to say that he wasn't equipped for the job, and if they went unsolved, that would create an open campaign issue that could be used against him throughout the election. "I know. Time is of the essence in so many ways."

"Then we have to be on our toes this weekend, and with a little luck, we'll see a nugget of information that will give us our next lead."

James bit his lower lip. Something had to break pretty damn soon or they were going to lose their chance. This case would end up like so many others in a file somewhere, unsolved, and the victims would see none of their property. They might end up with a new sheriff as well, and that would be because James failed to get his case solved. He was no stranger to pressure, but he was really beginning to feel it now, the weight of it pressing down on his shoulders.

"Is there anything else we can do right now?" Mattias asked.

"No. I need to talk to him some more, but I can't until he's feeling better. I figure we can change and have dinner. Then I'll call in to the hospital before we go to this charity thing you've roped me into." James tried to smile in order to carry off his tease, but his heart wasn't in it.

"ARE YOU sure I should actually wear this?" James asked as he stepped out of his bedroom in the tuxedo jacket. "I look like a dork."

Mattias flashed him an annoyed look and reached up to redo his tie. "That's because you have the tie upside down." He smiled and stepped back. "You do not look like a dork." Mattias led him into the bedroom and closed the door. "See? You look amazingly handsome." Mattias folded a silk square and placed it in his pocket. "Just a little more color and everyone—and I mean *everyone*—at the event is going to want to be seen with you."

"I'm sure that isn't true," James mumbled, resisting the urge to tug at his collar.

Mattias came around in front of him and did something to the front of the shirt and suddenly the pressure eased. "There are stretchers in the collar, but it was stuck."

"God, that's better." James smiled, and Mattias straightened his shirt.

"Go put on your shoes while I finish getting ready." Mattias patted him on the shoulder before leaving the room, and James carefully put on his shoes, trying not to wrinkle… anything. By the time he was ready, Mattias came out of the room he was using, a vision.

"Love the purple," James said.

"The vest is lavender and the tie is eggplant," Mattias corrected.

James stood, smoothing his jacket, and joined Mattias.

"You look amazing, by the way. The red is perfect, and you fill out that tuxedo as though it was tailored for you." Mattias flashed him a look that raised sweat under his collar.

James turned away to give himself some breathing room. Damn, how did Mattias manage to get him going with just a single look?

"So do you. That color is amazing." He resisted the urge to feel the vest, motioning to the stairs. He got his coat from the hall closet and threw it over his arm. The air was still warm during the day, but he figured the temperature would continue to fall in the evening and he might want it later. Mattias didn't seem to need one, and they left the house together and got into the car after locking the house.

"Where is this little soiree?" Mattias asked.

"It's at one of the buildings at Dickinson College. They've purchased a number of buildings over the years. Some of them are spectacular mansions. Apparently one of them is being used for the benefit." James started the engine, adjusted the comfort level in the car, and headed out of town.

"So what do you think we can expect?" Mattias asked.

"Well, I've never been to this kind of thing before, but I bet the heads of the college will be there, and the mayor of Carlisle will probably attend. That sort of crowd also attracts judges and a few other dignitaries. If you get one, you usually get others, and this is a charity that people in town feel strongly about. The theater was built in the golden age of movies and was bought a number of years ago by the Carlisle Theater Association. They've restored the inside, and it's absolutely stunning. They want to redo the outside and take it back to its original appearance. The town council and locals are thrilled about the idea. It will create a downtown centerpiece that will help set Carlisle apart. They want to create a live theater venue." James smiled.

"Somebody has been reading up," Mattias said.

James nodded. He'd figured it would be best to know what was going on. It would give him something to talk about at the benefit while he was watching people. "Yeah. My head is good for something other than a place to hang my hat." He figured a little self-deprecating humor was probably a good thing.

"I never thought you were stupid. Not for a second." Mattias smiled at him.

"Well, that's good to know."

"Do you know any of these dignitaries?" Mattias asked. "We want to be there, but it's best if no one knows you. If people are introducing you around as a police officer, that isn't going to help us."

"I doubt it. I don't run in those circles. So, while we're at it, what is our cover?"

Mattias chuckled evilly. "We are designers and work in interior restoration. We heard about the project, are extremely interested, and had to support the cause." He grinned, and James rolled his eyes.

"How about we live in the area, love the theater, and are thrilled to be able to support their efforts? Short, simple, and easy to remember." James knew keeping any story simple and close to the truth was the best choice.

"Maybe. But I like mine better. It has style." James didn't stiffen when Mattias patted his hand. "So we'll be friends, then? Or something more?"

"How about you and I just be us. We leave out the cop part and just be ourselves. Don't make too big a thing of it. It's a party, and we'll have a good time, mingle, watch as many people as we can, and hopefully discover someone with their fingers in the cookie jar." Something had to happen sooner rather than later.

He came into Carlisle and found a parking spot a few blocks away from the venue. The area was really full, and they walked across the tree-covered campus to the stunning yellow brick former mansion, where light poured out of elegant stained-glass windows. The building was beautiful, and after handing over their tickets at the door, they passed into elegant surroundings. Once again James wanted to tug at his collar simply because of his discomfort. Mattias, however, stood taller and seemed to fit right in.

Mattias took his arm and turned to him. "Isn't this amazing?" he asked as he half escorted James right into a conversation group. "Good evening," Mattias said as he accepted a glass of sparkling wine from a server. "I'm Mattias, and this is James." He smiled as he made eye contact with each person in the group. James had spent much of his career meeting people, but this was completely new, and Mattias was so bold.

"I'm Gladys, and this is my husband, Reginald," one of the ladies said with a smile. "We just love the theater and go every week." She leaned close to him. "He and I get dinner and then sit in the very back row to watch the film." She glanced at her husband.

"You never watch the film," one of the other ladies in the group said, turning her nose slightly upward. "The two of you neck like teenagers."

The group laughed lightly. This was obviously not news to any of them.

"Well, maybe James and I will have to join you one of these weeks." Mattias tilted his eyebrow in that way he had, and Gladys snickered.

"A little eye candy," Gladys said, teasing Mattias right back. "How exciting."

"So, I'm not enough for you anymore?" Reginald kidded, and Gladys shifted closer to him, taking his arm. The two of them had the look of teenagers in love. It was wonderful.

"Mattias and I have never been to one of these before," James said, hoping for a little newcomer sympathy and even a little gossip. It was clear enough that people had truly pulled out the stops. Gladys wore a sparkly lizard broach that was undoubtedly real jewels and caught the light each time she shifted.

"Oh, sweetheart, Reggie and I are old hats at these." She smiled as she looked around the room. "There's the mayor and his wife, talking to a couple of council members. I don't know the other people in their group, but the Hansens are here. He's the president of the college. Just take your charming selves over and talk to them." She took a glass from a server and sipped as Reginald guided her in the direction of the food.

"Shall we?" Mattias asked. "Groups will shift about all night, so let's mingle."

"I thought we were supposed to be watching people?" James whispered.

"We are. There's a couple standing over near the wall. They seem to be watching as well. So mingle and meet as many people as you can." Mattias smiled. "There's enough glitter in this room to attract a thieves' convention. Some of it is fake, but there's enough real stuff to make someone stand up and take notice. Come on." He led him into another group and made a quick introduction. "Did I hear you were on the home tour tomorrow?" Mattias asked. "James and I are volunteering to help." Mattias must have bat-like hearing, because James hadn't heard anyone say a thing about the tour.

"Yes. I'm so excited. The historical society has been after us to open our home for years, but Mark and I were never in town before. This year it worked out."

"Which home is yours?" Mattias asked, bold as anything.

"We're the large stone cottage near Thornwald Park."

James took note as Mattias clapped his hands once in obvious delight. "I'm one of your volunteers. How exciting. I've driven past your house many times and just love what you've done. It's stunning."

"Thank you. We love it."

"I can't wait to see the inside," Mattias said, and they talked for a while about landscaping and interior design as though they were old friends. It was amazing how quickly Mattias seemed to be able to put people at ease.

After a while, Mattias guided them to the appetizers and nibbles. James grabbed a plate and began loading it up because he was starving.

"Just take a little. This isn't the Golden Corral." Mattias took a few pieces of the finger food and stepped away. James went with him. "Eat slowly, and don't get anything on you." He winked and took a few bites, emptying his plate, then set it on one of the nearby trays. "Once you're done, go meet people." Mattias smiled and walked away in the direction of the wall-flowers they'd seen earlier.

James did his best to talk to people, but he didn't have Mattias's charm and easy manner. He was too much of a cop and used to interviewing and question-ing people, not engaging them in conversation about the weather or whether the windows were Tiffany. He nabbed another glass of wine and nursed it as he did his best to watch people without looking like he was watching. He was probably failing anyway and was immensely relieved when Mattias returned. "Well?" he asked.

Mattias sipped his drink. "Not sure. We'll keep an eye out." Music started from the other room. Mattias tugged him in that direction. "There's dancing."

"I don't dance," James growled under his breath, then finished the wine and set the glass aside. "We're here to watch people, not mix and mingle."

"Sure we are," Mattias countered. "Look, half the ladies here have on enough jewelry to attract attention. But see over there? The people I was talking to and the couple on the other side of the room, they're both just watching, not mingling, and when I approached, they tensed and seemed immediately uptight. Why come if you aren't going to enjoy yourself?"

"Maybe they're a little shy?"

"At two hundred a ticket? I don't think so," Mat-tias quipped, and James swallowed wrong, coughing slightly to try to cover.

"They were that much?" he asked.

Mattias waved it off. "Come on and dance with me," he said, taking James's hand and leading him to-ward the music. James was still surprised enough that his protest died on his lips. Before he knew it, Mattias had him on the floor with a number of other couples, holding him close enough that James could smell Mattias's subtle cologne.

"I'm terrible at this," James whispered, but Mattias simply pulled him closer.

"You're doing just fine." Mattias met James's gaze. "Dancing is like making love, only standing up and with your clothes on. You're damn good at that, so dancing should be a piece of cake." Mattias slowly flowed with him around the floor.

James was afraid they would become a spectacle, but no one seemed to be paying them any adverse attention. He finally relaxed and let Mattias lead. Once he let go of his self-consciousness, what Mattias had said sank into his brain and he actually felt his cheeks flush.

"You're a real silver-tongued devil. Is that how you got so good at your former profession?" James asked, and immediately felt Mattias tense and then misstep. James closed his eyes, wishing he'd learn to keep his damned big mouth shut.

When he opened his eyes again, Mattias's expression was hard, and a hint of fire blazed in his eyes. James needed to figure out a way to get well and truly past the idea of what Mattias used to do for a living. After all, a man's past was just that. James had one as well. Neither of them could change it, and yet Mattias's stuck in James's conscience and he wished to hell it would simply go away.

"Sometimes you can be a real ass," Mattias finally said.

"No argument there. Everyone is good at something." James wagged his eyebrows, and thankfully

Mattias relaxed as the song came to an end. They parted, and the music changed to something with swing. James shifted to the side of the dance floor while Mattias began to move. One of the ladies approached him, and he took hold of her arms, the two of them easily getting into the upbeat rhythm.

James knew he should be watching the people watching Mattias and his stunning partner, but he couldn't take his eyes off Mattias for a second. His jaw set, and James forced himself not to grind his teeth.

"I take it you don't dance like that," Gladys said from next to him, and James shook his head. "That's a pity."

James nodded his agreement, but could barely look away as Mattias deeply dipped the woman, her face splitting into a smile, her eyes as ravenous as James felt.

"He's only taking her for a spin."

"I know." He hated the idea that he was jealous. It was a waste, and he had no damned right to be.

"Sweetheart, I don't think she has anything he's really interested in." Gladys patted his shoulder, and James realized he needed to school his expression.

"I...."

"Don't worry. He looks at you the same way you look at him." She smiled, and finally James turned to her. "You boys, you think everything is such a big secret. I know love when I see it. Reginald and I have been at it for more than forty years." She turned, giving her husband the same smile James had seen on Mattias's face when he was picking on him. "Don't you worry. A dance is sometimes just a dance."

The music came to an end, and Mattias and the woman thanked each other.

Gladys nudged him in the side. "Go get him, tiger." She laughed as James found himself propelled forward without thought or volition. He simply went, took Mattias in his arms, and it was his turn to lead where he wanted them to go. He might have been clumsy when it came to dancing, but Mattias didn't seem to notice or care.

"I thought you didn't dance," Mattias said, delight dancing in his eyes.

"I don't. You're lucky I'm not stepping on your feet more than I am," James retorted. "And you know we're supposed to be watching people instead of having half the party watching us." He tugged Mattias a little closer. "If I try to watch while we dance, I'll get dizzy."

"Then settle down and stop moving in a circle." Mattias took back control of the dance. "That's much better." He seemed to settle into a slow rhythm, and James was more comfortable with his leading. "Are you watching people?"

James felt sheepish. "No," he whispered, his attention focused on where Mattias's hands touched him. Yes, he should be doing what he came here for, but he was way more interested in the rich scent that filled his nose and the way Mattias lightly brushed up against him as they moved.

"Me neither," Mattias breathed. "It's a little hard—okay, a lot hard, if you have to know the truth—to concentrate on anything other than you." He laid his head on James's shoulder, and James sighed softly, holding Mattias in return, just letting him and the music fill his attention.

James breathed easily, and for a few minutes, let go of the cop and the need for control. He could simply be himself and stay in the moment… at least for a small while. He spent so little time actually just enjoying things. He let the side of his head press to Mattias's, his hands gently caressing his back as the music continued to play. The DJ seemed to understand that if he wanted people to remain dancing, all he needed to do was play slower music and the dance floor stayed full. He caught Gladys's eye for a second as she and Reginald moved by. She flashed him a smile and then returned to her own dance-floor romance. Damn, she was a lucky lady to have someone look at her the way Reginald did, after more than forty years. That was special.

James tried to imagine if that could be possible for him. He was pretty sure that wasn't going to happen if he didn't take a chance of some sort. But playing with risks wasn't in his nature. James like things he could see and touch. And love… that had always felt like something nebulous that he couldn't quite put his finger on.

"Just relax and stop worrying about whatever has you preoccupied," Mattias said without letting him go.

"I'm fine."

"You're getting broody, and that isn't good at a party. Besides, we're supposed to be having a good time."

"I believe we were to be watching people."

"Can't we do both?" Mattias countered.

James had no argument to that. Sometimes it pissed him off that Mattias always managed to get the last word. Still, he relaxed and let go once again. Mattias was right. There was no harm in having a little fun.

The song ended and the music grew silent. James stepped back, and he and Mattias left the dance floor. James got a glass of water and stopped by the buffet, doing his best to watch the other guests. Mattias had been right behind him, but James found himself alone with the munchies and made the most of it. He was truly starving, and the small-bite sandwiches were good, so he made short work of six of them before anyone else came in the room.

"James," Mattias said, taking his plate and setting it aside. "I have something you need to see." He led the way down a short hall to where the coats had been hung. James paused outside the room as Mattias put a finger to his lips. He peered around the corner as a teenager went through the coats, placing things in his pocket.

"I don't think you want to do that," James said, grabbing the kid enough to unbalance him. He tried to pull away, but James had him on the ground in seconds. "I'm a police officer, and you've stuck your hands in some pretty deep trouble." He turned to Mattias, who was already on the phone.

"Help is on the way," Mattias said, then knelt down. "What do you think you were doing?" He tugged the kid's hands out of his pockets, sets of keys falling on the floor. "I take it you intended to liberate a few of the cars."

"I ain't saying anything," he snapped.

"You don't have to. Stealing someone's car keys is tantamount to stealing the car, so we can get you on a whole list of charges."

"I just wanted to have a little fun," the kid, who couldn't have been more then eighteen or nineteen, told him, his bravado gone.

"Looks like the fun is over before it even got started," Mattias said before lifting his gaze. "I'll meet the officers so we don't make a huge production that interrupts things too much." Mattias left the room, and James held the kid until two deputies arrived to take him into custody.

James had a deputy stay in the cloakroom to help anyone who might be missing their keys get them back. It seemed as though the party was over for them. James gave Mattias his keys so he could get home, and left with one of the other officers. James had to go to work, but Mattias might as well stay and have fun, though James longed to be able to stay with him.

CHAPTER 9

MATTIAS HADN'T been sure if James would want him in his bed, but he took that chance and woke in the night with James pressed against him. Mattias remained still so he didn't wake him, listening to James's gentle breathing. God, this was contentment at its best. It was hard for him not to wish this could continue forever. He sighed at the ease with which he seemed to trust James. Maybe it was because of their shared past... of a sort, anyway. But he doubted it was that. James was a solid, good, funny guy who didn't take offense at Mattias's teasing and even gave it back. That meant a lot. He'd always had this sense of humor that had driven his foster families crazy. James seemed to get it, and judging from his smile, he might even like it.

"Why are you awake?" James mumbled. "The grinding of the rusty gears in your head is deafening." His hand slipped slowly up and down Mattias's belly. "It's late, and we have to get up early."

"I know. I can go to the other room if I'm keeping you awake."

James growled and held him a little tighter. "You're warm, and it's chilly out there. Don't leave me without my furnace." He buried his face in Mattias's neck, his throat rumbling as he kissed him.

"I wish I could turn off this brain of mine, but I keep running over everything in my head." What really kept his mind churning was James. Mattias didn't want to think about what would happen once these thieves had been caught and this case was over. Damn it all, he'd always kept his heart to himself. Things were so much easier that way. He'd learned that lesson pretty quickly after losing his grandparents and being shuffled from foster home to foster home. If he grew to care for his foster family, they just rejected him for something he did, and he ended up moving on, so he stopped caring. That made the inevitable rejections so much easier to take. If he didn't care, then he couldn't be hurt.

This… whatever it was with James was different. The man got under his skin, burrowing deep before Mattias even realized it. Hell, he'd known him for less than a week, and already he was worrying what would happen when things ended.

"I know a couple ways to stop you from thinking." James pushed him forward.

"What are you doing?" Mattias asked as he stretched out, sliding his arms under the pillow while James slithered down his back, heated licks and kisses pulsing their way down him.

James mumbled, cupping his butt. "I was a little peckish and thought I'd eat out."

Mattias gasped as James parted his cheeks and buried his face between them. His brain short-circuited, unable to process the wickedly naughty delight that raced through him. He clamped his eyes closed, holding the pillow, doing his best not to scream his passion and wake the entire damned neighborhood. Not that he cared, as his attention zeroed down to the places where James touched him.

Nerves fired as wet, molten heat raged through him. He moaned softly in the pillow, his body shaking, pressed back.

"Are you all set for me?"

Mattias whimpered as he nodded. He was so ready, he could barely see straight. His body shook with anticipation, and he was only just aware of James getting prepared. Then he slowly pressed inside, and Mattias thought his head was going to explode. He opened his mouth to cry out, but no sound came, stolen away by the sheer ecstasy of James.

"Am I hurting you?" James whispered, pausing.

Mattias couldn't really talk but managed to reach around and tug James forward until he got the message to continue. "Don't stop…," he moaned softly as James slowly rocked back and forth. Mattias spread out, giving himself and his pleasure over to James. He wished he could see him, look into his eyes, but damn it all, that would mean stopping… and to hell with that. He turned his head to the side, and James leaned over him. Their kisses were sloppy, lips grappling between rocking thrusts.

"Have no intention of stopping until you're worn out." James rocked faster, holding Mattias around the chest, their bodies coming together as James stripped away the last of Mattias's control. Not that he cared. His pleasure was in James's hands, and he certainly seemed to know what to do with it. Mattias cried out, stilling as his release barreled into him, taking him over the edge with enough force that he saw stars twinkling behind his eyes like the night sky.

Mattias collapsed forward, with James resting on top of him, his lips caressing Mattias's shoulder. He didn't want to move for all the money in the world. This was bliss, pure and simple. James had shown him passion and a piece of himself Mattias never knew existed. Being taken out of his own head for a while had been a sublime experience that Mattias hoped would be repeated again and again.

His doubts niggled at the edges of his brain, trying to work their way back into his mind, but he held them at bay. They had no place there right now.

When James withdrew, Mattias slowly lifted himself up, reddening at the mess he'd made. He slipped out of bed and to the bathroom to wipe up, and when he returned, James pulled the fresh linens down. They got into clean, crisp sheets, James holding him just like he had when Mattias had just woken up.

"Now let that mind of yours settle on that for a while."

"Umm-hmmm." Mattias sighed, snuggling closer, and James held him a little tighter. Mattias finally closed his eyes as fatigue and contentment washed over him. The afterglow carried him into slumber's blissful embrace. He could be content and happy without worrying about the rest, at least for now.

When he woke in the morning, James was no longer in bed, and Mattias wondered if he might have dreamt it, but his scent still on the sheets told him that James had indeed been there. Mattias got up and dressed comfortably, then followed the scent of coffee down the stairs to where James spoke on the phone rather urgently.

"No, I don't think he's part of this. Just some opportunist," James was saying.

Mattias nodded blearily, poured a mug of wake-up juice, and settled into a chair. Last night's event had not happened at all how he'd envisioned, and he was disappointed, but watching James pace in the light sleep pants that clung to his hips and the T-shirt that stretched over his shoulders and chest was nearly enough to make him forget all about it.

"Yes. We'll be on it. The plan hasn't changed, and we're working multiple angles," James said, then listened and eventually ended the call.

"The sheriff?" Mattias asked, and James nodded. "He's getting nervous, isn't he?"

"Yes. Things were active for a while, and now they're quiet. He's afraid that with all the publicity, they may have left town and we'll never catch them. The latest polls show the race for sheriff tightening, and that's got Solly even more nervous. He's wanted this job for so long, and every time he gets close, something happens to yank it away."

"Did you get anything out of the kid from last night?" Mattias sipped his coffee and let it do its job. He needed to be able to think straight.

"He's some local kid who was stupid enough to think he could borrow someone's car for a joyride." James leaned against the counter. "It was nothing at all related to this." He scratched his head lightly. "I just want to go back to bed for a few hours and try to sleep, but I have work to do."

"What about the man in the hospital?" Mattias asked. "Is he okay?"

"Yes. I intended to see him last night." James put his mug on the counter. "I need to see him this morning before we go to the home tour thing." His shoulders slumped as he turned away. It was clear that James felt a little beaten down, and Mattias wondered what he could do to help.

"If it's worth anything, I doubt they've left yet. They need a score, something to propel them to their next destination. Yes, they've stolen a number of things, but none of them are enough to let them move and set up shop, even if they sold them all, and I doubt they have or the market would be flooded and we could trace things back to them more easily." He knew deep down that they were still out there. His instincts and what he already knew about them told him they were lying low for a bit, watching and looking.

"You really think so?" James asked.

"Yes. Relocating takes a lot of money, and if we're right, quite a bit of upheaval, especially if they have kids." He caught James's gaze as he nodded. "I bet you moved a few times growing up."

"Yeah, we did. It was a long time before I realized why." James yawned. "I wouldn't wish that on any kid."

Mattias sighed. "That doesn't mean they're going to stay very much longer, though. As soon as they make that score, they'll be gone, the kids pulled out of school, and wherever they're living left empty with a landlord wondering where they went." Mattias grew anxious himself. "All we need is a single break, and we can find these people." He sighed as he continued thinking while James drank the last of his coffee and turned to leave the room.

"I'm going to change and then head to the hospital. I need to talk to our victim to see if he remembers anything else. I'll be back in time for us to be at the home tour." He hurried upstairs, and Mattias sat alone, drinking his coffee, before going upstairs to get dressed himself.

"Do you want me to go with you?" Mattias asked from outside the bedroom door.

James opened it, standing shirtless in the doorway. For a second Mattias's mind short-circuited, but he got it together. "It's not necessary. I don't know how much he could tell us. You stay here and rest for a while. I'll get this done and then come right back." To Mattias's surprise, James stepped forward and kissed him. It probably shouldn't have shocked him given the fact that they had been sleeping together for the last couple of days, but James was in work mode and....

Mattias held James for a few seconds, kissing him in return before stepping back. "You need to go right now or both of us are going to be very late for everything today."

James shrugged on his shirt. "I'll hurry as quickly as I can. The tour doesn't start until two, so we need to be ready to go by one. That should give us plenty of time to repeat last night." James seemed to put it in high gear and was still bouncing a little as he left the house.

Mattias watched him go from out the back window, wondering if he could allow himself to think that this could possibly be real. He had to be realistic. He and James were very different, and it was pretty plain that no matter how Mattias acted or what he did, James wasn't going to be able to move beyond his past. This was a little fun, and once the case was over, Mattias would go back to Philadelphia and on to his next client. It didn't matter that the thought left him empty. He couldn't change what was in James's heart or what had been ingrained in his mind.

He turned back into the kitchen and put the dishes in the sink. He was about to go up and change when a ding caught his attention. He followed the sound to where James had left his phone on the counter. He picked it up and hurried out the back, intending to try to stop him, but James had left already, and as Mattias went back inside, the phone dinged again, the messages appearing on the screen. They were from James's mom.

Is your father there with you? It was immediately followed by another. *I got a voice message from him, but it was left from a 717 area code.*

Mattias nearly dropped the phone, but placed it on the table, doing his best to ignore the nagging feeling at the base of his neck. James's father was a thief—it didn't take a huge leap for Mattias to suspect what could possibly be happening.

He went upstairs and undressed, telling himself that he was jumping to conclusions. James's father could easily have picked up a burner phone that happened to have a number with James's local area code. He quickly showered and dressed, but the sense of dread didn't abate at all. Something was going on, and Mattias needed to find out what it was. If James's father was behind this spate of robberies somehow, then James was going to be put in a terrible position. The thought left Mattias cold. James had built a life for himself, one that was aboveboard. He was a good cop—honest and surprisingly caring.

"Shit," Mattias said out loud, then hunted up his phone to make a call. "Carrie, I really need your help...."

"WHAT'S THE problem?" Carrie asked as she breezed into a coffee shop on the main street a block from James's house where he'd asked her to meet him.

"Remember how I asked you to see if you could find anything out about James's father?" He tried not to let the edginess he was feeling creep into his voice.

"Yes. I called a few friends who owed me a favor. He's got quite a reputation." She ordered a coffee, and Mattias asked for a decaf. He'd had enough caffeine already and was going to fly out of the booth if he drank more.

"It's possible he could be here." Mattias leaned over the table, explaining the messages he'd found. "What if he was behind putting this ring together?" Maybe he was leaping to conclusions, but he needed her opinion. "Stranger things have happened."

Their conversation paused as the server brought their coffees, then resumed once she had left.

"Maybe they have, but that would be a real shit move," Carrie said.

Mattias smiled. She didn't pull any punches—never had.

"Yeah, it would. But, man, it would rip James to pieces. He deals with what his dad does through distance. It still bothers him, though…. I know it."

"I don't know what to tell you. You really care for him, don't you?" Carrie asked, and Mattias sipped from his mug, watching her over the top of it. "It's okay, you don't need to answer me. You wouldn't be bothering if you didn't give a shit." Now it was her turn to stall, and Mattias drank his coffee, knowing Carrie would tell him what she wanted to in her own time and not a second before. "My source, who's been around a lot longer than either me or you…," she said, lowering her voice. "There are rumors that he might be in the area."

"All right," Mattias agreed. He knew how these things worked, and if he wanted more, he was going to have to pay. Not that Carrie would be the one charging him, but the money would flow back downhill. Thieving was like the plumbing business—the crap ran downhill... most of the time. "James seems to think his father is after a last big score. Why would he be here?"

Carrie patted his hand as though he were being completely obtuse. "Because if he's caught, he's probably counting on his son getting him out of trouble. Like I said, it's a complete shit move, but it seems he's getting desperate. One big score will let him retire, and he can walk away free and clear. The problem is that no one ever does that. They get pulled in because someone wants something, and if you know where the skeletons are buried, you can get whatever you want." She continued drinking the coffee, making a face every once in a while.

"I need to find him," Mattias said. "I need to talk to the man." He needed to get word to him to back off. "I'll pay what I need to, but I have to meet him face-to-face. Is that something your source can arrange?"

Carrie set down her mug. "I don't know, but I'll try. Give me a day or so, and I'll get back to you." She patted his hand once again and started to slide out of the booth.

"I hate that I'm getting sucked back into this stuff." He'd left this life behind some time ago, and while he had no intention of taking anything, the shadowy life he'd known for so long seemed to be beckoning him once again, and it was scary that he could fall back into it with so little effort at all. The road to hell was paved with good intentions, and Mattias hoped he wasn't on the four-lane highway heading in that direction.

"READY TO go?" James asked as soon as Mattias arrived back at the house. "We need to get you down to your station so they can go over things with you, and one of the ladies called a few minutes ago. There seems to be some trouble with setting up the booth, so they asked if I could come early to give them a hand." James smiled with happiness, and Mattias didn't want to ask about the texts or anything else right now.

"Give me five minutes," Mattias said as he hurried upstairs. He quickly changed his shirt and grabbed a sweater in case it was chilly. Then he joined James in the living room. "How did it go at the hospital?"

"He's feeling better but doesn't remember much more. However, Kim called from the school. She asked if we could meet this evening, so I invited her to dinner. She wanted to talk, and maybe she'll have something for us."

So that was the source of James's excitement. "That sounds promising. Do you want to cook or should I?"

"Let's try doing it together?"

That sounded pretty amazing to Mattias.

James opened the door and held it for him. "Do you want to follow me or ride along?"

"It would be best if I had my own car since we're going to different locations," Mattias said before climbing into his car. He closed the door and almost got out again to tell James he'd changed his mind. He missed James's company, but knew he was being dumb. Mattias was going to have to get used to doing things alone again once this was over.

He followed James into Carlisle and then went out to where he was supposed to guide. He messaged James that he was there, then got out of the car and headed around to the house and then up the drive. Mattias rang the bell, and the lady from the party last night answered it.

"I was hoping it was you," she said with a smile. "Sarah Danross."

"Mattias Dumont. It's very good to see you again." He moved inside as she motioned.

She closed the door and stepped back as though the splendor of the interior was supposed to blow him away. It was gorgeous, with arched doorways and stone accents. Very much in keeping with the house exterior.

"This is lovely." And it was, but the wall colors were too strident for his taste, as were the draperies and furnishings. It was like she was trying too hard and consequently went overboard rather than just letting the home speak for itself.

"Thank you."

"What would you like me to do to help?" Mattias asked as she led him through the home. He paused in the dining room, where the table was set with china, crystal, and plenty of silver. This home was a casing thieves' paradise.

"I have the house ready. I was hoping you could stand between the dining room and the living room." She seemed a little frazzled. "I had only asked for one docent because my brother and sister-in-law were supposed to be here, but my niece got sick and they can't come."

"It's no problem." Mattias looked over both rooms with a critical eye for valuables. "Is there anything you want me to tell people as they come through?" He let his gaze fall over the living room, with its period crafts-man furniture and two Tiffany lamps, as well as other art pieces. He knew exactly what she had and wondered if he should tell her it might be best to place some of the more valuable things out of sight. But then she went through fluffing pillows and turning on the lamps. She was clearly meaning to impress and probably wasn't going to take Mattias's advice. Besides, he was sup-posed to be a helper, not an antiques expert. It was best to keep his mouth shut and his eyes open.

"The house was built in 1919, and it's very much of that period," she said.

"I can see that. The fireplace is massive and perfect for the room. I love the windows on either side. Are they original?"

"Yes. We kept as much as we possibly could. The dining room built-ins are mostly original. One of the doors was broken and we had it restored. But otherwise all the embellishments to the home are as they were when it was built." She did some last-minute fluffing and then stepped back. Sarah had obviously done a lot of work, and she was proud to get the chance to show it off.

"That's very good. It will give me something to talk about as people come through to help make them feel welcome."

"Wonderful," she said, then hurried out of the room toward the kitchen as a timer sounded. "I was baking some cookies for the guests and…."

"Sarah," Mattias said as he followed her. "Not for the tour?"

"Why, yes… I…." She paused as she took the cookie sheet out.

"They will end up strewing crumbs and grinding them in the rugs. I wouldn't put them out. It will make things much less of a mess. The last thing you want is chocolate fingerprints on your chairs," he cautioned. "Don't worry. You've done a beautiful job. Just relax and try to enjoy the day."

"Thank you." She set the cookies out to cool and began putting the ones covering the counter away. "But what do I do with all these?"

"Once they're cool, you could bag them up and give them out to the volunteers. I'm sure they would appreciate them." He left her to figure out what she wanted to do and got himself situated in the living room. Mattias wandered through the home to check it out so he could answer questions, grateful that people weren't going to be going upstairs. That way they could control the flow of people through the house more easily. Thankfully, one of the ladies from the historical society arrived and explained that she would watch the front door. Sarah decided to place herself toward the back of the house just as the first home tour patrons arrived.

Mattias texted James to check in with him and then went to work. He talked to the guests, explaining about the house even as he watched them, noticing who was paying particular attention to the contents of the rooms rather than the house itself. Most people fell into the second group. They asked plenty of questions about when the home was built and how much restoration was done. There were a few who seemed much more interested in what was on display. Mattias paid attention to them, as well as those who seemed to pay very little attention to much of anything.

He sent a few messages to James and received a few to alert him to the people to watch out for. About halfway through the tour, he pulled out his phone and sent James a message as one of the wallflower couples from the charity event walked into the house. They clearly had tickets and came right through to the dining and living room. Mattias could almost see their eyes widen and could hear the addition being done in their heads. Mattias managed to get a quick picture of the couple, adding it to his message before he went into his now rather rehearsed explanation of the room.

His phone vibrated, and he pulled it out to check the message. *Hold them there if you can. I'm on my way.*

I'll try, Mattias answered, then began talking about other items in the room and even inquired of Sarah if she had ever seen a ghost in the house. He was running out of items to talk about when James came through the front door. He kept his distance, and when the couple left, James went out with them. Mattias didn't know what he was doing, but stayed at his post, continuing to watch the other people as they came in.

He saw nothing especially suspicious after that, and made a few more notes that he texted to James so he didn't forget them.

By the time the tour was over, Mattias was tired and talked out.

"Thank you for all your help," Sarah said, handing him a big bag of cookies. "You definitely deserve these."

"Thank you." He hadn't meant for her to give them to him, but Mattias was grateful. He got ready to leave and met James out on the sidewalk.

"I followed them to the car and took down the plate. I had it run, and there was nothing unusual. It wasn't like I could question them. But I have a name and driver's license with all the associated information.

If they become of interest again, we can find them and see what they were up to."

"Did you see anyone suspicious at the ticket booth?" Mattias asked.

"Not really."

Mattias nodded. "You are going to want to have patrols set up near the house I was at. That place screamed 'Rob me. I have plenty of small, portable wealth.' The house may be the best bait we could possibly have. It's full, and I mean *full*. I could walk out of there with two people, their arms full, and hold hundreds of thousands of dollars in easily cashed merchandise that once it got to New York or Los Angeles would be nearly untraceable. There are three Tiffany lamps alone that are worth in the area of fifty grand each, and one that was stunning and probably worth a quarter million. It would take three minutes tops to get in, take what I wanted, and get out without anyone knowing." He was being as honest as he could with James.

"They have an alarm," James said.

"That would take a minute of that time to overcome… no more. I'm saying we need to protect those people from themselves." Mattias knew he had James's attention. "She put out all her best things on display for anyone to see. It's a miracle no one tried to steal anything during the tour."

James shook his head quickly, taking a few steps and then turning back around. "You have to be kidding me."

"I'm not."

He sighed. "Then it looks like we are going to need to set up a stakeout." He looked about as thrilled as Mattias had been the last time he had his teeth drilled. "I hate those things, but I have to agree with you." He walked up and down the walk before heading toward Thornwald. "They could pull in here, park, and go right into the yard through that growth. Then into the house. No one would see them if it was dark. This area is shaded from the streetlights, and if the car they used was anything other than white, no one would see them."

Mattias nodded. "Exactly." He walked farther. "What's back there besides houses?"

"There's a drive into the park area, but the way is barred."

"By what?" Mattias asked, and James swore under his breath. "Let me guess, a chain that can be opened because people need access."

James nodded. "They could hide back there and get in that way."

"Not if a temporary construction barrier of some sort were to go up. Say a Jersey barrier. You have to have some of them. Have one delivered, with a sign saying that the road is going to be under construction. It can stay there for a week or so, right?"

"I need to call the sheriff," James said, pacing away from him. Mattias let him talk while he explored the area a little more. He ended up leaving the park by the back way. There were houses lining the other road and most of them had fences, so that way was going to be problematic at best. No, if given the chance, thieves would take advantage of the darkness to make their move. His instincts screamed it. Mattias continued his circle, returning to where James was on the phone.

"You and I need to go back, right now," James told him softly when he was done with his call. "Solly is going to have Clay and Pierre come to the house, and we're going to figure out how we can do this. I'll meet you there." James took off at a quick walk, and Mattias got to his car.

By the time Mattias arrived at James's house, he was the last, and hurried inside to find James cooking and talking, with the planning already underway.

"There's an apartment building just down the street on the other side. We should be able to park in there and have a good view," Pierre was saying.

"Yes. But we can't just sit in cars there," Clay took up. "People live there, and the last thing we want is for them to call the police. Granted, we can head things off with Carlisle PD, but if they can see us, so can others."

"There's a van we can use. It's for transport but has windows in the back. They're tinted, so we can park it and watch from the back," James offered. "Mattias and I have a meeting in an hour. I'll call Briggs and get his permission. You two take the first watch. I doubt anything will happen while it's light...."

"I heard Sarah talking before I left, and there's a chance she could be away tonight or tomorrow. Her parents need her. So when the house is empty is going to be the thieves' best shot... and ours." Mattias wished he'd remembered that earlier, but it was fine.

"I'll make a call. You go pick up the van and call here when you're in place. Don't draw attention to yourselves. The purpose of having you there is just to make sure we don't miss a time window." James took a pan off the stove and set it on the back burner. "Mattias and I will take over about ten. If anything does happen, call for backup right away and don't let them leave. We're only going to get one shot at this, so we want to make it good."

"We know," Clay and Pierre said before bundling out of the house in a hurry.

"That didn't take long," Mattias said as he sat down.

"They're good guys and know what to do. The department will have the van ready, so all they'll need to do is pick it up and drive it over." James sighed. "Stakeouts are the most boring part of this job. Most of the time, you wait and wait, hoping you aren't wrong and that what you expect actually happens. A lot of the time it comes to jack squat." He turned back to the stove but didn't seem to be doing anything. "What if all this effort comes to nothing?"

Mattias got up and walked up behind him. "Then we'll follow whatever leads we have. Don't doubt yourself now." He wound his arms around James's chest to try to reassure him. Or, the more he thought about it, Mattias might have been comforting himself as well. He was the one who had suggested they watch the house, and now a great deal of resources were being allocated to it. What if he was wrong and this whole home tour idea was way off base? He had no way of knowing if the thieves had even been on the tour. Mattias closed his eyes, resting his head on James's shoulder.

"I know, but I keep wondering if we're making huge leaps in logic," James said.

Mattias nodded. "Yes, but we have to get ahead of them. Waiting for the next robbery and hoping they make a mistake isn't going to get us anywhere. It certainly isn't going to help the sheriff with the election. We have to try to get out in front, and that means taking chances—following hunches and intuition to try to look into the future to see if we can think like them. It's a leap of faith of sorts." He released James even though he could have stayed like that for hours. "What can I do to help with dinner?"

"I figured something simple, but my head is in other places," James admitted, so Mattias checked what he'd done and took over from there, finishing the potatoes while making a salad. When the bell rang, James got it while Mattias sliced the beef he'd cooked under the broiler and dished up.

"I'm sorry for having you come so far," James was saying as he led a lady into the kitchen. "This is Kim Miller. Mattias is an associate of mine."

Mattias shook her hand, and James offered her a place to sit.

"I really appreciate you calling me back."

"I nearly didn't," she said as Mattias set a plate down in front of her. He then put one at James's place as well as his own before taking a seat. "There are two children that meet the description you gave me. I can't tell you their names or give you much information. I have to protect their privacy."

"We understand that," Mattias said as he took a bite of the well-seasoned beef. "But we need your help."

"Yes, I know. One of the teachers heard one of her students talking to the other kids. This particular boy is quiet, small, and when he does talk, speaks with a southern accent. The family just moved here recently, and the kids started a few weeks ago." She took a few bites and smiled. "This is really good. Thank you. My husband is away on business, and I had planned to go in to work tonight. It's been a while since someone cooked me dinner."

"Kim…," James said rather plaintively.

She reached into her purse, which she'd placed next to her chair. "This is the address we have on file. The only reason I'm giving this to you is because of the things my teacher heard. They were concerning enough that we thought someone needed to look into them. Apparently one of the first-graders told his teacher that he had to go to work after school. When she asked if he meant doing chores, he shook his head and said he worked with his mommy and daddy. Under normal circumstances we probably wouldn't think much of it, but last week his arms were scraped, and he said it happened when he crawled through a doggie door." She set down her fork and took a drink of ice water, clearly more than a little upset. "My first concern is for those kids. If they're being used for something wrong, then it needs to stop. It must stop."

James took the piece of paper. "If these people are involved, then we will do our very best to make it stop and see to it that the kids get the best help we can give them."

"I know." She took another few bites. "I'm protective of my kids, and I have to think of them first."

"Of course you do," James said. "I have some wine if you'd like some?" They probably should have offered earlier, but she declined and continued eating.

"You have to promise me that if this family isn't involved, the children aren't going to get hurt."

"We'll be discreet and very careful. I can promise you that," James said even as his eyes did a little dance. Mattias could tell James was itching to make a few phone calls to get things rolling. But to his credit, he stayed where he was until they finished eating. Kim, however, was still a little nervous.

"You did the right thing," Mattias told her. "James is a good cop. He'll investigate before he does anything." Mattias was sure of that, but the story Kim had told them sounded exactly like the people they were looking for. Mattias's heart beat a little faster, and he was ready to hop into action as well.

"If we suspect that our kids are in danger, then we have to report it, but it's always a matter of weighing things against privacy and what's best for the kids." She had a tough job, there was no arguing with that. It was pretty clear that she cared for her students and wanted to help them as best she could.

"I'll do my very best. I never want to hurt innocent lives. That isn't my goal. But if these people are using kids in their robberies, we need to get the kids out of that environment and into a place where they can be kids and have a chance at a better life." James shivered, and Mattias knew it wasn't the temperature in the room. It wasn't hard for Mattias to imagine James putting himself in the position of those kids.

"It's possible they have nothing to do with what we're working on," Mattias said, knowing it was true, but hoping this was a solid lead that would allow them to finish the case. Though the end of the case meant the ending of whatever was between him and James, and that wasn't something Mattias was ready for.

"I almost hope it does," Kim said. "These two kids… they're always tired, and when you watch them, you know they don't have things easy. Their teachers both say that they sometimes fall asleep in class, and at lunch they eat up everything they're given and are the first ones done every time. The teachers have taken to keeping granola bars and things in their desks that they can give the kids." She swallowed and shook her head. "Sometimes our teachers… they provide whatever their kids need. It's a hard job, gentlemen, because most of them care almost too much about the kids in their class."

"We'll do what we can. I can promise you that," Mattias said around the lump in his throat.

Kim met his gaze, and for a second, he felt completely exposed. Then her principal's gaze moved on, and Mattias breathed a sigh of relief. It was like being back in school again and she knew what he was thinking. "You understand about these kids," Kim said, and Mattias nodded.

"So does James," Mattias added. "We will do everything we can for them if their parents have them involved in this." The thought of those kids being hurt and forced to rob for their folks took away Mattias's appetite. If it was true, he wanted to string people like that up by their ears. His grandparents had loved him. At least Mattias had had that to remember during the years afterward.

"Thank you." She finished her food and pushed back the chair. "I have to get home, but thank you for the dinner, and please let me know what you find out." She stood and picked up her purse, clearly as shaken as Mattias felt at the moment. "If there is something I can do to help those kids, please tell me."

Mattias and James stood as well and walked her to the door. "We appreciate your help."

She paused at the front door, turning back to them. "I only hope that's what I've done. The kids in my school, all of them… they're part of me. I try to help each of them as best I can, and so do the teachers." It had clearly been a difficult decision for her to contact James.

"You did the right thing. James will handle this as delicately as anyone possibly can. He's very good, and like I said, he understands. If these kids are being used as part of these robberies, he will be able to help them." Mattias turned to James for reassurance and received a nod in return. "You did the right thing, Kim. I promise you that."

She smiled slightly, nodded once, and then left the house.

Mattias closed the door and locked it.

"Finish eating, Mattias. Then you and I will check out this address and these names before meeting Clay and Pierre. Bring that computer of yours along. We may need it."

They finished their dinner, and Mattias helped with a quick cleanup. He packed what he thought he was going to need and met James in the living room with his bag, then followed him out to the car. Mattias drove while James made phone calls. When they reached Carlisle, James directed him to the address Kim had given him.

"Is that it?" Mattias asked as he peered out the window at the house with missing siding, and plywood nailed to the outer walls. The front door and windows had wood screwed over them.

"That's the address." James parked the car, got out, and carefully approached what was left of the house. "I was afraid of this." He looked all around, but other than a few passing cars on the street, no one stirred in the house or in either one of the neighboring homes, which weren't in much better condition. "Stay here with the car. I'm going to go around back."

Mattias didn't want to be left alone, but he stayed by the car, watching nervously as James disappeared around the rear of the house. That gave him a chance to be grateful that it seemed they had a false address. They were getting closer, though—he could feel it. But that meant a few more days with James were probably all he could hope for.

CHAPTER 10

JAMES RETURNED to the car and climbed inside. "No one has lived there in a long time." He'd been hopeful, but as soon as he saw the house, he realized Kim had been given a false address. That could very well mean they were getting closer and on the right track. On Monday he was going to have to talk to Kim and possibly watch the school to see how the kids in question got home.

"I'm sorry."

"It's part of the job." He sighed, "Come on. We need to get to the stakeout. It's getting late." His heart beat a little faster as some of the pieces of the puzzle began to fit into place. The thieves had arrived in Carlisle a few months ago, enrolled the kids in school to allay suspicion, and used a fake address. What Kim had said about the kids fit with the picture he had in his mind.

"What are you thinking?" Mattias asked before James could start the engine, placing his hand on his arm. "Clue me in."

"Just how helpless those little kids must feel. My dad is a thief, I know that. But he didn't bring it home, and he never involved me in a job." James felt half shattered, and Mattias leaned over the console, drawing him into an awkward hug.

"This case is hitting close to home for both of us." Mattias closed his eyes and sighed into James's ear. "We need to bring it to an end."

James's own emotions were stirred up, and for a second, he wondered if that was why he'd developed this attraction to Mattias so quickly. It wasn't like him at all, and he knew it. James wasn't the kind of person to trust easily, and Mattias, from what he knew, wasn't either. So why was this moving so fast? It could only be the situation, and maybe once it no longer existed, things would return to normal and the heat between them would cool.

Then James did something he'd rarely done in his entire life. He sent a silent wish out into the universe, a hope that this was truly real. But only time would tell.

"Yes, let's find out what's going on and bring this puppy to an end."

"HAS THERE been any activity?" James asked over the phone as he approached the area of the stakeout. He didn't want to garner any unnecessary attention, so they talked before he approached the van.

"No. The house is quiet. There were more lights on, but then some of them went out and a car pulled away. So I think the house is empty at the moment."

On one hand, that was good, because maybe the bait would be taken sooner rather than later. But there were no guarantees. "We're on our way. Mattias and I will walk there and take over for the two of you."

"Let's stop at a store," Mattias suggested, and James made a turnoff. Mattias hurried into the grocery store and came out with cold caffeinated drinks and plenty of food. Then James drove to where they were staking out the house, parked a bit away, and walked up around the apartment building and to the van.

Mattias opened the door and climbed inside, with James following behind, doing his best not to watch the way Mattias's pants clung to his backside. He was here to work and needed to try to keep his feelings for Mattias separate from the task at hand.

Mattias settled into the back seat, and James closed the door. "Anything new?" Mattias asked. The only light came from a streetlamp half a block away. The interior lighting inside the van had been disabled, so from the outside it seemed dark and empty. There was just enough to see the basic outline of things in the van. James hoped that would improve as their eyes adjusted.

"No. The house is quiet. No one has approached." Pierre handed him a set of night-vision binoculars. "There also hasn't been any activity from the side either. We figured it would be best to monitor the woods as well."

"Thanks, guys. You might as well go on home. Mattias and I will see things through for most of the night. Come on back in the morning, and we'll switch out. I'll call if there's any activity or if we need backup."

"You better. We want to be in on any action," Clay told him, with Pierre nodding his agreement.

"Okay. Get some rest. This could turn out to be a long one." James thanked the guys for all their efforts, and they left the van. He settled into a seat and tried to get comfortable as soon as the door closed. As James continued watching out the window, Mattias shifted from the very back seat to sit next to him.

Mattias pulled out his computer and darkened the screen to a minimal level. "What did you want me to try to do?"

"The address Kim was given was obviously bogus. But we have a name, probably fake, and a picture. There are a number of pieces, and parts of it have to be real, right? If the lie varies too far from the truth, then it's easier to spot. So take what we know and see if we can put it together and find anything that might be truthful."

Mattias chuckled. "You don't want very much."

"I know. I sent a message to Kim already and told her what we found. She is going to get me the names and the information she has on the kids. We have to keep that information private, but something about them has to be real." James was growing more and more frustrated.

"When you get me the information from Kim, I'll add it to what we have and see if I can come up with anything." Mattias got busy, and when James's phone vibrated with a message, he handed it to Mattias, who got the information and went to work in earnest while James continued watching.

Time went by with its usual slowness. Stakeouts were like that. Hour after hour of watching and waiting, hoping something would happen while sitting, eating, and drinking anything to help keep alert and awake. There were times, many of them in his career, that he had wanted to give up, but stakeouts were a matter of perseverance, and James had plenty of that.

"Have you found anything?" James asked as he scanned the area around the house with the night-vision goggles. He lowered them before turning to Mattias.

Even the dim light of the screen would be blinding with the goggles.

"Maybe. But I'm not sure. I didn't find any kids with that name in the area. So I was a little stumped, but then I started looking at the homes in the neighborhood of the address that they gave us, and I came up with something interesting...." Mattias paused as he continued typing.

"Hold it," James breathed. "I think we have activity...." He grabbed the goggles and scanned the area. "Yes...." He checked the time. It was nearly one, but James messaged the guys and made the call for backup. "I need you to stay here."

Mattias closed his computer and set it aside. "I'm going with you." Before James could tell him no, Mattias had the door open and was already getting out of the van.

"Stay here," James whispered between clenched teeth. "I can't keep you safe, and you're not trained for this." He knelt down, peering around the van, using the goggles to see more clearly. Two people were at the door on the side of the house near the back. It was clear enough that they were trying to get in, and it seemed to James that they weren't having much luck. He made another call. "Approach quietly. I want to catch them in the act," he told the dispatcher.

"Backup is a minute away," he received in response.

Sure enough, a car with no sirens or lights came around the apartment building, parked near the van, and two officers got out.

James motioned for them to be quiet as he continued watching. "They're standing near the door, and nothing has happened. We have to wait until they get inside." He wasn't going to let them get away, and for that to happen, there had to be a crime.

"There's a car on the other side of the park, as well as on the street behind it. Just say the word and everyone will move in."

James nodded to acknowledge the message, continuing to watch the back-door area.

"They've moved away from the door and are trying the window." It opened, and then one of the people lifted a kid. Well, holy shit—they'd been right. The thieves were using kids. Part of him had hoped he and Mattias had been wrong. The back door opened, and the two people disappeared inside the house. "Get everyone to move in."

James grabbed his gun, giving Mattias a hard look even as he got ready to go. The man was a stubborn ass, and James shook his head as Mattias stepped away from the van. James pulled him back.

"I'm going."

"You stay here where it's safe." He stared daggers at him. "I have the officers for backup."

"And I know how the thieves think," Mattias countered. "Now go get them. I'll stay behind you."

James wanted to wring his neck, but time was of the essence and he didn't have any more of it to argue with Mattias. He turned and took off across the street with the others, reached the back door, and signaled the others to cover the front and the sides. No one was getting out of that house and past them.

"This is the police," James called as he entered the house with two officers behind him. "Stop what you're doing and lie down on the floor. You won't be hurt." He looked both directions and made his way farther into the house.

"That way is the living and dining room. Then the hall and a room used as an office. The stairs are off the hall," Mattias whispered from behind him.

James wanted to turn and smack him, but a quick movement caught his eye, and he reacted by pointing his gun as a kid about seven ran toward him, his eyes wide, fear following in his wake.

"Get him out of here," James told Mattias, who scooped up the boy and hurried back the way they'd come. The kid never said a word, but James didn't think any more about it as he made his way farther into the house, gun at the ready.

A metallic crash echoed through the otherwise silent rooms. James carefully headed in that direction and caught a man and a woman at the top of the basement stairs.

They held up their hands. "Don't shoot," the man said shakily.

"Both of you, get down on the ground," James barked, and they dropped, their hands out. The officers with him from Carlisle PD handcuffed each of them and then pulled them to their feet, searching them for weapons before removing them from the house. Thankfully it didn't look like they had gotten very far, with just a few items piled on the dining room table, most likely getting them staged to carry outside.

James left the house, stepping outside into a hive of activity. Sheriff's deputies, Carlisle PD—everyone was there.

"Gentlemen," he said as he approached the two officers who had taken custody of the thieves. "Please deliver them to the sheriff's department. They'll take the lead since this is their case."

They looked like they were going to argue with him, but then nodded, and the deputies on the scene put the two of them in their squad cars to hold them.

"James," Mattias called, and he went over. "This is Claude, and those were his aunt and uncle."

"Where are your parents, Claude?" James asked.

Claude sniffed. "They're dead." He turned away, covering his little face as he broke into tears. "Are you going to take me to jail?" He continued crying, and Mattias put his arms around him and let him cry, meeting James's gaze with such pleading that James didn't know how to respond at first.

"We have Child Services on the way. Donald Ickle will be here in a few minutes," Red said as he cut through to him. "I went ahead and called him as soon as I saw a child was involved."

"Thanks," James said.

Red tilted his head to the side. "Who is that with the boy?"

"He's a consultant working with the department on this case." James didn't fill in any additional details. They weren't pertinent at this time. "Mattias and I will talk to Claude once he has a chance to calm down and Donald gets here." Donald Ickle was a kind of legend with law enforcement. His husband was a police officer, and somehow Donald always managed to make miracles happen for the kids in his care.

"Have the homeowners been notified?"

"Yes. They are on their way home now," Red said.

James nodded and joined Mattias and Claude. There was nothing more to do other than wait at the moment. James hated waiting, and thankfully, Donald arrived a few minutes later.

"This is Claude," Mattias said when Donald arrived. "He doesn't talk much."

Claude still held Mattias's hand and didn't seem inclined to let go.

"He told us his parents are dead and that he was living with his aunt and uncle," James told Donald.

"Okay." Donald knelt in front of Claude. "I'm Donny, and I'm here to help you." He held out his hand and waited, not moving any closer until Claude released Mattias's hand and took Donald's. "It's okay."

Claude's big blue eyes scanned over the three of them. "Are you taking me to jail? Auntie said if I make noise or anything, the p'lice would find me and take me to jail." He started to cry again, and James turned away, trying to wipe his eyes discreetly so no one would see him. Mattias handed him a tissue without saying a word, and was probably using one himself as well.

"You aren't going to jail. I have someone who is going to take care of you. And they will make sure you don't have to sneak into other people's houses again." Donald had such a gentle voice. "And I think you already know her." Donald turned as Kim Miller approached their small group.

"Mrs. Miller?" Claude's eyes seemed to hold a little less pain when he saw her. Clearly Kim was an amazing principal.

"Come here, Claude." She knelt, opening her arms, and he hurried over to her, dissolving into tears in her arms. "You're going to come home with me."

"What about Sissy?" Claude asked.

"Her too." Kim turned to Donald and explained that Claude had a sister. "Do you know where she is?" Kim asked, and Claude pointed behind the house.

"There's a little girl in the car the perpetrators must have used," Clay told him quietly. "She's locked herself in the car and won't come out."

"Let's go with Mr. Donny and get Sissy. Then you can both come home with me." She released Claude and took his hand. "You're her big brother, so you need to be strong for her and help her not be scared, okay?" Kim asked, and Claude nodded solemnly. Clay took Donald, Kim, and Claude around and back toward the car.

"God…," Mattias said as he put away his tissue, eyes still shining in the filtered streetlight's glow. "I wasn't prepared for that." He seemed unsteady on his feet, and James gently patted his shoulder.

"Go on back to the car. I'm going to need to wrap some things up here." All he wanted to do was go home and slip into bed, but that wasn't going to happen, not for a while.

"Clay and I can take them to the station, get them booked and sitting in a nice cell for the night. We can separate them and let them stew before we talk to them," Pierre offered. "It's been a very long day, and trying to question them when we're tired isn't going to get us anywhere. The jail is loud and noisy, so my guess is that neither of them is going to get much sleep, so they'll be more ready to talk." He flashed a quick smile, and James nodded. That idea was sounding better and better by the second.

"All right. You stay with them until Clay comes back. I want to make sure the kids are settled and things are finished here." James sighed, relieved some things were wrapping up as the homeowners hurried up the walk, demanding answers.

"Sarah," Mattias said with a smile. "The police are still working inside, but I believe we got here in time." He smiled and some of the head of steam she was under abated.

"You're a police officer?" Sarah asked.

"No. I'm just working with them as a consultant. Detective Levinson can answer any of your questions." Mattias stepped back, and James did his best to fill her in while keeping her calm until the teams were done inside. Then James took her into the house to verify that nothing was missing or damaged.

THE TIME seemed to get away from him. There was so much to do, but eventually the house was secured and statements taken from the homeowners. The crime scene team finished their work, and the two suspects were transported. Claude and his sister, Justine, were taken in by Kim, with Donald following. The other officers left the scene, and James headed to his car, half dead on his feet, the adrenaline of the chase and capture having faded long ago.

Mattias sat in the car, the window partially lowered. "If I smoked, I think I'd have created enough clouds for a thunderhead by now."

James knew exactly how he felt, and nodded once he was in the driver's seat. "At least those kids are with someone who will care for them." James had no doubt that Kim would look after them and see the two of them through this very rough time.

Mattias didn't answer, staring out the window. James started the car and drove back to his house. They rode in silence, and that was fine. The air was heavy, as were the thoughts that ran through James's head.

Finally, he pulled up in front of the house, not a word spoken between them.

James snapped open his seat belt and got out of the car. "Come on. Let's go inside."

Mattias followed, seemingly on autopilot.

"Do you want something to drink?"

"Vodka," Mattias said, the first words since they'd left. "A lot of it." He sighed. "But that's a shitty idea." He slumped down on the sofa in the living room.

James got some water and handed Mattias a glass when he returned, sitting next to him. "That sucked. I wish we'd been wrong."

"Yeah. Me too. Seeing those terrified blue eyes...." He turned to face James, and for a second, he saw that same fear, like he'd just lost his grandparents again. James didn't know what that kind of loss felt like. He still had his parents, but he understood pretty clearly that those little kids had been taken advantage of and manipulated. They needed a chance to be away from that. "Their parents are gone, and the people who were supposed to love and protect them just used them for their own gain."

"They won't be able to do that again. I intend to make damned sure of that." James was already listing some of the charges that could be leveled against them. Breaking and entering was the least of them.

"Yes. But now those kids are in the system. Yes, they're young, and there's a chance they could find a stable home and be adopted, but there's also the chance that they'll be shuffled from place to place the way I was." Mattias's shoulders slumped. "And I know there's nothing I can do about it."

"It makes you think of what you went through, I know that." James shifted closer. "Sometimes you do your job and things work out. Other times there are things you can't do anything about. Regardless of what happens, those kids have some time ahead of them before they are free for anything. Whatever custodial rights their aunt and uncle have are going to take time and court hearings to terminate."

"Yeah, I know. Kim and her husband are going to be good foster parents for them." Mattias sighed, and James scooted closer to him. "I know I'm being way too emotional."

"Hey. Your feelings do you credit." James was pretty certain that Mattias was showing part of himself that he didn't usually wear on his sleeve. This vulnerability was a sight for him alone, and it touched James's heart in a way he didn't expect. He put an arm around Mattias's shoulder and let him lean on him. Separating himself from the job and the people he encountered was part of his profession and training. He reminded himself that Mattias hadn't had that same training. "Right now, the best thing we can do for those kids is to get to the bottom of this whole thing. That means making sure their aunt and uncle can't use them again… as well as finding out what we can about these thieves so we can put all of this behind us."

Mattias nodded. "But what happens when this is over?"

"Well… I guess you go home." It wasn't what he wanted, but James was practical.

Mattias nodded and sat back up straight. "I suppose." He blinked and got to his feet. "I think I'm going to go on up to bed." He drank the water James had brought him and took the glass to the sink. Then Mattias climbed the stairs without another word.

What was he supposed to do? James hadn't been expecting to find someone he'd grow so close to. This entire situation was out of control, and yet it felt so damned right that it was frightening. The logical part of his mind said that he was doing the right thing, but the rest of him ached to go up those stairs and take Mattias in his arms and never let him go. This wasn't how things were supposed to happen. People met, they dated, got to know each other, had sex, grew closer, built trust. All those things were supposed to take time—not happen in under a week. He held his head in his hands, trying to get the damned thing to cooperate, but it wasn't happening.

James locked the doors and turned out the lights before going up the stairs. The last few nights he'd found Mattias in his bed, and what gloriously happy nights those had been. Regardless of what had happened during the day, their snark and teasing, the nights had been spectacular. Hell, if James were honest, he preferred the snarky, "stand up for himself" Mattias to the one who quietly went up the stairs. At least he knew how snarky Mattias felt.

The door to Mattias's room was closed, and James felt shut out. He stood outside the door, listening for a few moments, but everything was quiet. He thought of knocking or even trying the door, but that was too dramatic for words. He ended up turning around and going to his room, where he dressed for bed, cleaned up, and then pulled back the covers to get in.

"What the fuck am I doing?" James asked himself in a whisper. He wasn't a drama queen, and damn it all, he wasn't going to get what he truly wanted if he simply gave up. That was so not in his nature. James dropped the covers back in place, marched across the hall, and knocked on the door. This was a moment of truth, one of decision.

The doorknob turned and then the door opened. Mattias stood in the doorway, the light from the bedside lamp spilling out into the hall. The broken expression in Mattias's eyes was too much for James to bear. He stepped forward, framing Mattias's cheeks in his hands, and brought their lips together in a kiss that nearly stopped his mind.

James poured everything he had into that kiss. He had one chance to tell Mattias that he wanted him. Practicality dictated that Mattias go home when this was over, but James didn't want him to. He had no idea at all what he… they were going to do, but he didn't want this to end. He pressed Mattias back into the room and over to the bed. They fell together, with James ending up next to him, the mattress bouncing slightly. Mattias wound his arms around him, holding tightly, the energy James poured into the kiss coming right back from Mattias, amplifying and then flowing back and forth again and again.

"Are you sure about this?" Mattias finally asked.

James stopped. "I'm not sure about anything, but I know I want to figure it out. And when this case is over, I don't want you to go away. I want to see you again and go on dates… do all those things that people do when they're falling in love." There, he'd said it, and he felt so much better for it. "Is that what you want too?" James asked.

Mattias nodded, and James smiled, then kissed him once again, and the energy between them rose higher and higher. Clothes ended up on the floor, on the nightstand, wherever they fell, as James and Mattias celebrated their initial understanding. James was happy, and he let that happiness bloom and carry him on wings that let him soar for hours until they were both too tired to move, falling asleep curled around each other and not stirring until morning and work forced them to part.

CHAPTER 11

MATTIAS WAS just as happy as James appeared to be. Dang it, James practically whistled as they got out of the car, heading into the station. Mattias followed behind, enjoying the view with a smile on his lips, practically dancing up to the building. As they got inside, Mattias's phone rang, and he fell behind to answer it.

"Hi, Carrie," he said quietly.

"It took some time, but I got a message to the person you wanted to speak to," she said seriously, and his smile faded. He'd almost completely forgotten about James's father. "He is in the area, as you suspected. There's a coffee shop next to the courthouse in Carlisle. He'll be there in an hour, and if you want to see him, you should be there then."

Mattias nodded to himself. It looked like the case that had brought him here was coming to an end, and he debated whether to take the meeting or not. But if the accomplished thief was up to something on James's territory, he needed to know about it and do his best to put a stop to it. He wasn't going to have him ruining James's career for some selfish reason. Mattias cared way too much for James to let that happen. "I'll be there, and thank you."

"You're very welcome." Her tone lightened. "You owe me a nice lunch for this."

"You got it." Mattias smiled as he ended the call and went into the station. "Where are James and Pierre?" he asked as he set his bag on the table in their workroom.

"They're talking to our prisoners. They have them in separate rooms and are seeing what they can get out of them." Clay was using his own computer, most likely typing up reports.

"Do you have any idea how long they'll be?"

"A couple hours at least. These things take time and never go as quickly as you see on television. I made sure they knew their rights last night, and they've had a chance to stew over what happened." He lifted his gaze. "The jail was particularly noisy last night because of some suspects that were brought in at about two, so it's likely our pair didn't get much sleep."

"I see."

"Not that we had anything to do with it, and it wasn't planned, but James and Pierre thought it best to see if they would talk this morning."

Mattias nodded as Clay went back to his reports. He knew James was anxious to get any information he could out of the thieves, and he wasn't really surprised that he and Pierre had already gotten to work. "I have a meeting downtown in a little while. So would you please tell James that I'll be back in a couple of hours?" Mattias was damned nervous about this meeting and wanted to get there early so he could scope out the coffee shop before James's father arrived.

"I'll tell him," Clay said.

Mattias left the station, hurried out to his car, and headed downtown. The drive was a matter of a few minutes, though finding parking took longer, and Mattias fed the meter with all the quarters he had before going inside and stepping up to the counter. He ordered a regular cup of coffee, sat down at a table, and pulled out his laptop for something to do while he waited.

It wasn't as long as he expected before a man who had to be James's father walked through the door. The brightness in the eyes and the chiseled jaw were too distinctive for him to be anyone else. Mattias caught his eye, and he came over. "Elias Levinson," he said.

"Mattias Dumont." They didn't shake hands, and Elias sat down across from him.

"I'm only here because I'm curious why you'd want to talk to me. I did some checking on you, and I know what you do and your past. I also know that you're working with my son." His gaze was hard as flint, and Mattias was well aware he was in the presence of a man who had been hardened by life and would do what he had to in order to get what he wanted.

"I'll come to the point. I want to know why you're here." Mattias met that hard gaze with steel of his own.

Elias's eyes narrowed, and he inhaled, then released his breath but remained silent.

"James has to suspect that you're here," Mattias said. Though they'd never spoken about it, James had to have seen the text messages from his mother.

"And what business of yours is my relationship with my son?" Elias asked. "You work with him as some sort of consultant…." He sneered at the end of the sentence as though Mattias had turned his back on some sort of brotherhood of thieves. Which couldn't have been further from the truth. There was no honor among thieves—Mattias was well aware of that, and so was Elias, he was sure. If he was here in town and he was planning something…. Mattias swallowed with the realization that Elias could very well be here because he was behind the rash of burglaries, and that this was his retirement plan.

"And you're in town because you're hoping for one last big score." Mattias pushed his cup forward and leaned over the table. "I have sources too, and if you did any checking, then you know I have a reputation." He leveled his gaze at Elias. Hell, he should probably have told James he was coming here and blow the whistle on his father. The last thing he wanted was for James to get hurt, and with Elias in town, there were so many scenarios that could cause just that.

"Yes, you do," Elias said tersely. "Which was why I agreed to talk with you. I was curious about what you wanted with me. Now I have a pretty good idea." The way he tilted his head sent a chill up Mattias's back.

"You don't give a crap what your presence here will do to James, do you?" Mattias challenged. It was time Elias knew that James had someone to watch his back.

Elias met his gaze. "I have one last score, and then I'm done. James will understand that I can set him and his mother up for the rest of our lives. I can quit, and she and I can live quietly in retirement. But I can't do that otherwise. They don't have Social Security for guys like us." Elias looked at him as though he was supposed to understand, but Mattias simply shook his head.

"Go get your score someplace else. I'm going to give you until tonight to clear out," Mattias told him flatly. "You better be gone and on your damned way back to Florida, or I'll be on the phone to a contact at the FBI, letting him know where you are and just how easy it would be to find you." Mattias wasn't playing around. "And so help me, if I find out you're at all involved in the case he and I have been working on, I'll turn you over to the police so fast that it will make your head spin."

Elias smiled. "Oh yeah? And what about James? Will you put him through that? Having to publicly deal with his father, the thief? Is that going to help him?" The man was devious and fucking selfish as hell.

"It's sure as hell better than you not getting caught." Mattias slipped off the chair. "You seem to forget. The son isn't responsible for the sins of his father, and if I had to bet, I'd say that James would handcuff you and take you in himself if he had to." He'd heard enough. He got his bag and turned toward the door, but Elias grabbed his arm.

"You may just get to test that." Elias tilted his head toward the door as James pulled it open and came inside.

Mattias felt the floor threaten to open up and swallow him the instant he saw the stormy look on James's face leveled his way.

"What are you doing here?" James turned to his father. "With him?"

Mattias opened his mouth to answer, but James cut him off.

"Just go back to the station."

"James, I...." He tried to explain, but it wasn't going to do any good. Mattias closed the lid on his laptop and slid it into his bag, then turned and left the coffee shop, heading back to his car. He got about halfway there before he was grabbed and whipped around.

"Whatever you were cooking up with my father, just forget it." James growled softly, but with plenty of menace. "I trusted you, and then I find you here with him!" He shook. "Just get the hell out of my sight." He turned and strode back into the coffee shop.

Mattias trudged back to his car and started driving toward the station. He thought of going back to James's, getting his things, and leaving. The case was essentially over. They had caught the thieves, and the issue for the sheriff was past. He could call a news conference and crow that the department had helped make the county safer and that his opponent had rushed to judge while he spent the time to catch the real thieves… or whatever people said in order to get elected. Mattias nearly made the turn to head to James's, but he didn't have a key to the house. And while he was up to the challenge of those special locks of his, he wasn't going to break into his house. James could think whatever he wanted of him, but Mattias wasn't going to prove those thoughts true.

At the station, he went into the room they had been using. Pierre and Clay sat in their usual places, talking quietly. "How did the questioning go?"

Pierre nodded and smiled. "They were ready to tell us anything to try to save their own skin. Apparently they're working with someone else, and they only confessed to some of the robberies. They told us about the woman and her partner who were selling the goods, and they even gave us an address. The sheriff has two deputies heading to Mechanicsburg to pick them up. Clay and I are trying to work out who the mastermind behind this whole thing is."

"Mastermind…," Mattias said, but kept his mouth shut about James's father. He wasn't going to raise more questions until he could get James to talk to him. This whole thing was a pain-in-the-butt mess, but he was going to bring it to an end, and then he might as well go home. He sat down and got to work himself.

"What did that keyboard do to you?" Pierre asked after a few seconds. "You're pounding it like it committed a crime."

"It didn't, but someone sure did." Mattias wished he'd said nothing and went back to work, hiding behind the screen. He typed more softly and then gave up. It was stupid, but the thought that James hadn't given him a chance to explain and hadn't trusted him or cared enough to ask why he'd been talking with Elias really tore at him, especially after last night.

He closed the lid on his laptop and turned to the wall to check the time. It wasn't even noon, but it felt as though he'd been up all day. Maybe having your heart broken did that to you. As Mattias thought, he was being stupid. Things with James had been moving quickly. Mattias had forgotten to keep his guard up, and this was what happened. He should have kept his distance and just done his job. But no, he had to get involved with the one man he'd let get under his skin, only to have the trust he'd started to build destroyed. Mattias should have known. This was how things worked for him. His parents, his grandparents, all ripped away when he needed them most. Mattias had just begun to think he could get past all that. Hell, he'd been trying to keep James from getting hurt. Well, no good deed went unpunished. He had never truly understood that saying until now.

"It looks like you all have things pretty well in hand," Mattias said, then swallowed. "I'll talk to the sheriff and probably be heading home tomorrow or so." There was no need for him to stay any longer. He had done what he'd been hired to do, and going home was for the best. Still, running away wasn't in his nature, and he was determined to have this out with James. Good, bad, or indifferent, he was going to have his say, and then he'd go home.

"We've still got plenty to do. Someone devised this whole robbery scheme and then got these people to work for him." Pierre handed him a printed report. "I'm just finishing up their statement, but they were brought here from Alabama some time ago and promised jobs and a better life. What they got was a job stealing."

"We're working to try to corroborate their story. It seems designed to tug at the heart, but I'm not buying it without some sort of proof," Clay said skeptically. "Still—"

"They used their niece and nephew to help them steal," Mattias interjected, and they both nodded. "I bet they claimed they were desperate and had no other choice." His anger grew. "They also said that they were afraid to tell anyone because their handlers would turn them in." He shook his head. "I could have written that script with my eyes closed." Mattias drew closer to the table. "Check them out carefully. You have every reason to be skeptical." He certainly was.

"You don't believe it either?" Clay asked.

"Nope. Sounds way too rehearsed, and I've heard it before. Make sure the kids are really their niece and nephew, and then pressure them about who is behind this. They know more than they're saying, and I'll bet they are hiding behind this sob story." Mattias was pretty sure of that.

He wasn't able to do anything more to help at this point. He couldn't go back and talk to them, even though he was pretty sure he could see through their story in a few seconds. All he ended up doing was checking the clock every few minutes, which was completely stupid. He'd already done what he could do, and the rest was basic law enforcement. The more he thought about it, the more he realized there was nothing to keep him here. Mattias stifled a sigh, packed up his things, told the guys that he was going, and left the building. His small apartment in Philadelphia was sounding better and better.

CHAPTER 12

JAMES YANKED open the door to the coffee shop after watching Mattias get into his car, and strode up to his father under a full head of steam. He calmed himself when he got halfway to the table, then plopped down in the chair that Mattias had occupied. "What are you doing here?" he asked more calmly than he'd expected to be capable of at the moment.

"How did you know where I was?" his father deflected. He always tried to take control of every situation.

"Mom messaged me because she wondered if you and I were together. It seems you called her from this area code." James leveled his gaze. "Then when I asked Mom where I could find you, she said you had told her you were here." His father was clearly learning that his mother was an easier source of information than he realized. "Don't be mad at her—I wormed it out of her. I am your son, after all." He couldn't help taking a dig at him. James loved his dad, but that didn't mean he wasn't angry with him as well. "So…."

"You aren't going to worm things out of me as easily as your mother," his father said flatly.

"Maybe. But I'm sure I have other ways of getting you to tell me what I want to know." James pulled out his phone and set it facedown on the table, near his hand. He was sending a message. "So… why are you here in town, and what were you and Mattias planning? Don't you dare tell me this is a trip to visit your son, because I know you better than that." His anger built at a steady pace.

"I wasn't planning to come here, but the trail I was on led to this area." His father leaned forward and lowered his voice. "I won't tell you about it other than I'm leaving town in a few hours. I haven't done anything, and you won't have to deal with me on your turf. And you can tell your gum-flapping mother that I'm on my way home." He sighed. "Things didn't work out."

James narrowed his gaze. "So… then, what were you and Mattias planning?"

He shook his head. "Nothing. He asked for this meeting and basically told me to get the hell out of town or he was going to make sure I paid for it." His father's gaze grew softer. "He threatened to let you know that I was here, and even pressured me with the FBI. I haven't seen anyone that worked up over something in a long time. He was even snippier than you get." His dad smiled broadly.

James felt the air whoosh from his lungs, and damn it all if it wouldn't go back. He forced air in and then coughed, wondering what the hell he'd just done with Mattias. "You mean you weren't planning anything?"

"Nope. The conversation centered on how he was going to run me out of town on a rail." He checked his watch. "Speaking of leaving, I need to go if I'm going to make my plane." He stood and was about to leave. "You know, but the next time our paths cross…."

"It's not going to happen, Dad." He motioned to the table, and his father sat down. "Don't come back here. The next time you do, I'll use everything I know against you, and don't think for a minute that I won't." He could finally breathe again. "My entire life I've had to deal with what you do for a living, and what I do and how I feel. I'm not going to do that any longer. So consider this a forced retirement."

"Jim, your mother deserves…."

James had heard this justification plenty of times, and he was no longer buying it. The last week had shown him just how much his father and his choice of profession had influenced his life, and he wasn't having any more of it. Hell, he'd jumped to conclusions about Mattias, and now… God knows what he'd done and what he was going to have to do in order to make up for his anger and the fact that he hadn't given him a chance to explain.

"No, Dad. Mom deserves to have you around and not in prison for the last years of her life. You've put her through a lot, and it's over. Whatever this score is that you're chasing… it ends now." He wasn't going to let his father walk out of there without saying what he needed to.

"I'm your father. You don't get to tell me what to do."

James blinked and took a calming breath, then picked up the phone. "I don't make idle threats, Dad. If you can't give it up for Mom, then she might as well learn to do without you now as opposed to later." He began dialing the station. "Let me talk to Ravelle," he said, and waited as he met his father's gaze, steel for steel. One way or another, this was going to end.

"Fine." His father lowered his gaze, blinking for the first time James could remember.

James waited on the line while his dad turned and left the coffee shop. He watched his dad go and finally breathed a sigh of relief before Pierre came on the line. "Is Mattias there? I need to speak to him." He hadn't been bluffing for a second, but it looked like he wasn't going to need to take the nuclear option, and he needed something to ask Pierre now that he had him on the phone.

"No. He gathered his things and left a few minutes ago. His computer and everything is gone," Pierre said. "He was talking like the case was over and he wasn't needed any longer. Also, the guys returned with two more suspects, and we need to interrogate them. They're in holding cells right now."

Shit. James really needed to find Mattias and explain what an ass he'd been. Damn it all, he'd let the crap with his father color the way he looked at Mattias, and it could cost him everything. "Okay, I'll be right there." He couldn't go back to his house right now. The round trip would take too long. Instead, he made sure everything was paid for and then hurried to his car and back to the station.

JAMES SPENT the next two hours talking to suspects, playing each of them off the other until a much clearer picture of what had been happening emerged. It seemed there had been a leader, and they had her in custody… but only through sheer luck. When the deputies had gone to pick up the two suspects, they happened on the third leaving the house, and when they called it in, she matched the description of the seller they had been tracking. Getting the story out of them was difficult, especially since the leader lawyered up immediately. But the others were willing to sell her out to save their skins, and James had a pretty good idea of how they were recruited and brought up here. Finally, he sat across the table from Ellen Mavle and her lawyer.

"It seems we have a very good case. The four people who work for you all turned on you." James grinned. "It seems you didn't engender any sort of loyalty. And now we have you as an accessory to child endangerment and abuse. That's going to carry as much time as the burglary and larceny." This was turning out to be totally beautiful.

"What's the deal you're offering?" the attorney said.

James chuckled. "You know I don't make any deals." He stood. "I don't even need her to make any sort of statement. I just wanted her to know that I hope she gets used to our accommodations. The DA is going to claim she's a flight risk, and given the fact that she's involved in human trafficking… she isn't going to be going anywhere." James tried to keep his head in the case and where it needed to be rather than on Mattias and where he might have gone. Every time he'd taken a break, he'd called, but Mattias hadn't answered.

"You think this is over?" she said, and James turned around. The attorney was already shushing her, but it seemed she was having none of it.

"Actually, I do," James said calmly.

She met James's steely gaze with one of her own. "I have information you'd like to know. How is it going to look for you when the world finds out about your father?" She cocked an eyebrow as she tried her best to smile.

James snorted, pulled open the door to the interview room, and walked out to the officers who had been
waiting on the other side. "Put her back in her cell."
He'd had plenty of dealings with the ramifications of
his father, and frankly, at the moment there were more
pressing issues on his mind.

He walked back down to the case room, where he
found Clay and Pierre.

"We have the arrest reports done. Is there anything
we need to type up from that last interview?"

James shook his head. "I think this ring of thieves is
over." He was about to turn to leave when Solly joined
them, smiling. James explained what they'd found and
who they had in custody. He also went through how
they'd caught the people and how Mattias had been a
huge help. He praised Clay and Pierre for their hard
work, and when Solly returned to his office, James followed him inside and closed the door.

CHAPTER 13

MATTIAS IGNORED yet another call from James as he sat in the diner a few blocks from James's house. The server refilled his cup of coffee while Mattias stared at nothing out the front window—until James hurried through the door.

"How long are you going to sit here?" James asked.

Mattias shrugged. "I don't know," he said softly. Then he put some money on the table that included a generous tip, stood, and walked past James to the door. He stepped outside and started walking down the sidewalk toward James's house, with James coming up behind him. "I assume that now that you're back, I can get my things and go."

"We got the ringleader. The woman who was trying to sell the goods," James said. Mattias didn't slow down and didn't answer. "The other four all fingered her, so the case is over."

"Good. Now I can get my things and go home. I did what I was contracted to do, and now I won't be darkening your doorstep again." His anger swelled more quickly than he wanted. Mattias had spent plenty of time thinking about what he wanted to say when he saw James. He had the words all set in his head, but now that it was time to say them, the words were gone, and all that was left was anger masking hurt.

James took his arm, and Mattias wrenched it away. "Don't be like that."

Mattias stopped on the street corner, close enough to his destination that he could see James's house. "Be like what? You dumbass. Hurt? Upset that you didn't even give me a chance to talk?" His hands shook, but he wasn't going to do this here. Anything he said wasn't going to change a goddammed thing. Still, he couldn't seem to stop himself once he got started. "I went there to warn your father off. But you barreled into that coffee shop and thought the worst of me. The entire time we've been working together, you never saw me as anything other than a thief… an extension of your father. And the first time that you seemed to get some sort of confirmation of that, you pounced." Mattias made a grand motion with his arms. "Well, you were wrong, oh mighty detective. You got it wrong." He stepped closer. "I was there because I cared enough to not want your father to make trouble for you. I know how it feels to have your loyalties split and to have them threaten to tear you apart."

James gaped at him. "Yeah… I get that now. And I was wrong. Dead wrong." He grabbed Mattias by the shoulders, but Mattias knew what was coming and pulled away. "I stood up to my father and told him to go home. Whatever he wanted here wasn't going to happen. I was ready to call the FBI." James swallowed. "I can't live with this constant division of loyalties. Not anymore." He placed his hands on Mattias's shoulders once again. "I know you were there for me," he added in a whisper. "I see now what I was doing. I know I was painting you with the same brush as my dad, and I kept doing it even after you proved to be a very different… a much better man."

Mattias's heart wanted to reach out to James, but he stopped it. That was what had gotten him into this mess in the first place. He'd let himself hope that James would see him as more than a thief, and James had proven on multiple occasions that he couldn't do that. Mattias's heart ached to believe James. Dammit, he wanted to, but he just couldn't take the chance. Not again.

"Just unlock the house so I can get my stuff."

James didn't move. "Can't we talk about this?"

Mattias didn't dare answer. His resolution slipped each second James looked at him. How in the hell had he fallen this far this fast? Those intense eyes and the pain he saw in them tugged at him, but he had to be strong. There was no way that James was going to see Mattias as anything other than his past. Mattias might have been that man once, but that wasn't who he was now.

Finally, James nodded and turned away. Even though Mattias had said that was what he wanted, the movement felt as sharp as a slap. Maybe he'd hoped James would put up a fight… or pull out some grand gesture to show how he really felt. Instead, he stomped over to the front door, inserted the key, and pushed it open before going inside.

Mattias bumped into James, standing just inside the door, when he stepped inside.

"What the hell are you doing in my house?" James asked, and Mattias leaned to the side as James's father approached both of them, a gun cradled in his hand. "And what the fuck do you think you're doing?"

"Come inside. Both of you," he said, waving the gun, and James stepped forward.

Mattias swallowed, wishing he could say he was particularly surprised.

"What do you think you're doing, Dad?" James asked, the anger washing off him palpably. "Put the gun away." It was pretty clear that James wasn't taking this seriously.

"I can't do that," Elias said, motioning to James. "Take out your gun and set it on the floor. Then sit down on the sofa." His tone was as serious as a heart attack, and James complied, clearly stunned. Mattias sat stiffly in the chair Elias motioned him into. "Now isn't this warm and cozy."

"What the hell are you up to, Dad?" James asked. "How dare you pull some stunt like this." He began to get up, but Elias walked over to James and placed the gun to the side of his head.

"This isn't a joke, and you need to sit still. It would be a shame if I had to tell your mother that you had been killed." Elias cocked the hammer, and James stilled completely, paling by the second. "Now that I have your attention…." He stepped back. "I have a few things to do, and because of your little stunt this afternoon, I can't trust that you'll leave me alone, so…." He pulled zip ties out of his back pocket and secured James's hands. Then he did the same thing around his ankles.

"Fuck, Dad, is whatever you're after worth all this?" James asked.

"It doesn't matter," Mattias said, turning to James. "This isn't something your dad can stop. I know he told you that he stole to support you and your mother, but a long time ago that became total bullshit. He loved

it. There's a rush—isn't there, Elias?" Mattias asked.
"You may as well tell him." He could read the signs
on Elias's face just as easily as on a junkie's in need
of a fix.

Elias kept quiet, tightening the tie around James's
ankles.

"You were the one behind all this, weren't you?"
Mattias asked. "You brought those people up from the
south to steal for you, and let me guess… you figured if things went wrong, James would get you off
the hook." He watched Elias closely as he reached for
another tie.

"That's enough out of you." Elias waved the gun
in front of him, and Mattias quieted. He snatched Mattias's hands, tied them together, and then did his ankles.
"You talk way too damned much."

"Why are you doing this?" James demanded. "You
really think you can get away with this?" He struggled
against the bonds for a second and then gave up.

"Of course I can." Elias set the gun on a table,
out of reach. "I need this last score, and I'm this close.
So all I have to do is get you out of commission for a
few hours, and then I'll be out of here and across state
lines." He seemed pleased.

"And in the meantime, you've decided to hold
your own son hostage," Mattias snapped. "What the
hell kind of father are you?" He got angrier the more he
watched the light dim in James's eyes. James had protected his father for years, and caused himself a great
deal of conflict in the process. He'd even put his own
career in jeopardy in order to protect him, and now…
this? "He's a shit father. Look what he's done. He went
to prison, and then got out and started stealing again.
Both your mother and you have paid for his decisions

your entire lives." Mattias didn't back away from Elias's gaze even after he backhanded him across the cheek. "See, the truth hurts. He doesn't give a damn about you or anyone else. He can say what he wants to justify it, but he gets off on the adrenaline."

"I did the best I could for James and his mother."

"Yeah. You subjected them to lives of insecurity and having a jailbird for a father and husband. And now rather than walking away, you hold your own son hostage… but with good reason." Mattias braced for another slap, but it didn't come. Instead, Elias grabbed the gun and brought it closer, pointing it right at Mattias's nose.

"That's more than enough out of you. Does he know the kind of man you are?" Elias sneered.

"Of course I do," James answered. "I'm not stupid. I know all about Mattias's past. He was strong enough to give up what you can't seem to—not for me, not for Mom." He kicked out, catching his father in the leg.

"Dammit!" His father backed away, swearing under his breath. His hand went back, presumably to slap James, but he lowered his arm, eyes still blazing.

"I used to believe all the crap you peddled, but not anymore. And I know Mom isn't going to either."

"Your mother will believe me," Elias spat. "She and I have been through too much together, and she deserves a quiet retirement."

"The only place Mom is going to be spending her retirement is in divorce court, or in prison on visiting days unless she decides she doesn't want to see you." James struggled with his bonds, but they were too tight, and Mattias was well aware they weren't going to break them. "Mattias is worth a dozen of you. He at least realized what he was doing was wrong and decided to change his life. That takes more courage and guts than you'll ever have." James held his chin firm and turned away from his father toward Mattias.

Elias's phone rang, and he glanced at the screen and then went farther into the house.

"What do we do?" Mattias whispered.

James shrugged. "He's my father. What is he really going to do to me?" He clearly didn't see the severity of the situation.

"And he's going to let you go and just go home and tell your mother that he held you hostage so he could get the remaining goods from the theft ring he organized?" Mattias raised his eyebrows. "Your dad has gone too far, and I think he knows it." Mattias wished he could reach out and touch him, hold his hand to comfort James… as well as himself. But that wasn't possible, and Mattias pushed the notion out of his head. He needed to keep his wits about him.

James sighed. "Yeah." He sniffed slightly. "We need to get out of these or get some help here, and fast. My dad took my phone."

Mattias nodded. "He didn't get mine." He winked. "I was a thief, remember?"

"Then where…," James started to ask, and Mattias shifted his gaze to his crotch. "You put it there?"

"Sleight of hand," Mattias said, shifting on the sofa, hoping he didn't break the dang thing as he tried to work it out of his underwear and into his pant leg. At least then it might be accessible. He managed to get it out from under his ass and down to the base of his calf, keeping it under his leg so no bulges would show. It was the best he could do as Elias returned, fuming under his breath.

"Where is all of it?" Elias asked, leaning over James. "What have you done with it?"

"All the goods? They're at the sheriff's station in evidence," James said levelly. "You'll never see any of it, and the rightful owners will get it back."

Elias must have gripped James's legs hard, because he winced but said nothing.

"What did you do, dig up the backyard?" Elias asked.

James just smiled. "I know you, remember?" James said, but Mattias got the idea he was running a bluff. Clay and Pierre hadn't said anything about finding the stolen property. So this had to be a way of getting the location from his father.

"I helped the guys log it all into evidence," Mattias offered to add weight to whatever story James was weaving. When Elias turned his visual wrath on him, James nodded and flashed a quick smile.

"Do you remember how I used to punish you?" Elias asked. "I can do that now."

James kept his cool and shrugged again. "There's nothing any of us can do." He held his gaze level even as a flash of fear crossed his eyes. Mattias hated that fear, and he hated Elias even more for putting it there. "I suggest you let us go and leave before it's too late."

Elias's phone rang again, and he groaned before leaving the room once more.

Mattias managed to get the phone out of his pants leg, then bent forward to get it between his hands and onto the sofa. He managed to get his finger on the button to unlock the phone and pressed the emergency button. "We need the police now," he said as soon as he heard an answer. Mattias gave James's address as Elias came back.

Elias snatched the phone away, throwing it across the room. The phone smashed on the fireplace hearth. "You son of a bitch!" Elias yelled and lunged for him.

James jumped off the sofa, barreling into his father, sending both of them sprawling onto the floor, knocking over the center table. Mattias leaped forward as well, adding his own weight as Elias sprawled under both of them. Mattias lay across Elias's legs and James did his best to pin his shoulders while Elias tried to reach for the gun, which had been knocked onto the floor. Mattias lunged upward, his body pinning Elias's arm and hand to the carpet just out of reach of the gun.

"What do we do now?" Mattias asked as he did his best to keep James's father from moving.

"It shouldn't be long now. As soon as the call was placed, the address of a police officer will show on their screens and…."

James grinned as sirens sounded, getting louder and louder, until they stopped right in front of the house. Lights flashed in the front windows, and soon police burst into the house, dozens of them. At least it seemed that way to Mattias. They took charge of Elias, with the sheriff following inside as soon as the scene was secure. He and James were cut out of their bindings, and Mattias rubbed his wrists, grateful for the freedom of movement once again. The officers helped them to chairs and fanned out throughout the first floor of the house. Elias sat with officers surrounding him as Mattias and James answered all their questions. As they were winding up, Sheriff Briggs approached where they sat.

"Sheriff Briggs," James said formally as he rose to his feet. "I'd like you to meet my father." He stood tall as he shocked everyone in the room… well, everyone except Mattias. "He's the one who brought our other five suspects to this area, and it seems he's the one who directed their actions through the woman we have in custody."

"Your father?" Pierre asked, sharing a glance with Clay.

"Yeah. And apparently the property they haven't tried to sell is in the backyard of the house we raided this morning." James turned to his father.

"You tricked me, you little—" Elias said as he was led out of the house.

"It wasn't hard," James called back, and turned to Briggs. "I think we're pretty much done here."

Mattias gently touched his hand to let him know he was there for him, and James lightly squeezed his fingers in return.

"All right," Briggs said, bringing all attention back to him. "I want both of you to come see me tomorrow." The best way Mattias could describe his expression was understanding tinged with discomfort. "In the meantime, you're going to have to answer plenty of questions. Some I'm sure you'd rather not."

Mattias had no trouble believing that.

HE AND James bade the last of the police officers goodbye a couple hours later. A few times, Mattias did wonder how many of their questions were necessary and how much was their curiosity and disbelief that they had just arrested the father of one of their colleagues. It seemed to Mattias that James had been honest and forthright about his relationship with his dad. Even Mattias had squirmed a few times at the questions, especially about what James knew of his father's activities, which seemed to be very little. Finally, Clay and Pierre, along with the local police, had gotten the information they needed, and James saw them to the door and closed it behind them.

"What a day." He went through to the kitchen and slumped into one of the chairs.

Mattias stood behind him, and James reached up to take his hand, squeezing his fingers.

"I'm sorry for being such a complete jerk." He turned, looking up at Mattias with warm eyes. "I should have asked you why you were there. Dad told me you ordered him to get out of town."

Mattias nodded. "He was going to hurt you—I knew it." He released James's hand and sat down. "I saw some texts on your phone from your mom."

"Yeah." James nodded. "I saw them too, and figured they were from a burner phone or something. Dad never came here. It was sort of our unspoken rule and how I managed to keep some distance from what he did." James took his hand again, his thumb making small circles on the back of it. "Then Mom texted again about a meeting my dad had at the coffee shop. I came there to tell him to get away, and I saw you." James sighed. "I knew he was here for no good, and I confronted him after you were gone. I…." James shook his head, then reached for a napkin from the holder on the table and used it to wipe his nose. "I didn't really think he was behind all this."

"I suspected him as soon as I saw the texts. He's your father, though, so I guess I didn't want to think he'd do that. But then again, the man I met in the coffee shop was anything but fatherly."

James nodded. "He actually got this idea and put it into action here because he thought I'd be able to cover for him if it went bad," James mumbled. "I could never do that. He might be my father, but I have more integrity than that."

Mattias brought James's hand to his lips. "I think we all understand that." His throat felt like sandpaper, and Mattias swallowed hard. "And I get why you were angry with me, but you should have talked to me. I trusted you—opened up to you—and you know how hard that was."

James hummed softly. "I think we both have issues in that area. I trusted you too, and thought you had betrayed me. Instead, you were proving that my trust was well founded, and I didn't listen." He squeezed Mattias's hand once again. "I pretty much suck at talking about my feelings. Both of us tend to hide behind snark and teasing. But this is from the heart—stay.... I don't want you to go."

A lump formed in Mattias's throat. "I have to for a while. I have other clients and bookings coming up." He sighed. "But I travel a lot, and I can pretty much base myself out of anywhere." He met James's unusually subdued gaze. "But I know what you're really asking... and yeah, I want to give this a shot, you and me."

"Then that's enough for now. I don't even know if I'm going to have a job tomorrow. The fallout from this whole thing with my father is going to be epic, and the news is going to have a field day with it. Especially if my father decides to turn it into a media circus."

"Then we'll figure it out," Mattias said quickly. James turned, smiling at him. "And if things don't go well, then we can go back to Philadelphia, and you and

I can work together. I've helped more than a hundred departments across the country, and I have a dozen departments who want me to work with them. We can do it together." Even as Mattias offered, he knew it was unlikely James would want to do that. In his heart he was a police officer, and that was what he really wanted to do. Mattias couldn't blame him at all.

"Thanks," James said, pursing his lips slightly before leaning forward to kiss him. Heat built quickly, the way it always seemed to when James was close. But something was different this time. James's touch seemed more intense... or maybe it was because they might have finally figured it out—or at least made a good start. If Mattias was going to give him his heart, he knew James would cherish it, just as he cradled James's within his own.

"Do you want something to eat?" James asked.

Mattias stood, still holding James's hand. "After," he whispered, and James followed, letting Mattias guide him up the stairs and to the bedroom, the one they had shared for most of the time that Mattias had been there.

James stopped him at the door, smoothing his fingers through Mattias's hair. "I gave you my heart some time ago, and I thought you had taken advantage." James put his hand in the center of Mattias's chest. "Instead, it found a custodian who was willing to go out on a limb to try to protect it."

"I know what you're saying." Mattias placed his hand on top of James's. "We'll figure it out. Whatever comes our way, you and I will figure it out."

"Is that a deal?" James asked, a wry crook to his lips.

"You better believe it. And I always get the better end of the deals I make. So, what are you offering?" Mattias cocked his eyebrows and didn't suppress the smile. "Hot sex?" he asked, and James nodded. "Understanding?" Mattias smirked. "Asking before you blow your top and embarrass yourself?"

James snickered. "I'll try."

"And love?" Mattias added, going for the gold ring.

"Definitely. Lots of love. I think that and the hot sex go together. Do you want to test that theory?" James wound his arms around Mattias's neck, drawing them closer.

EPILOGUE

MATTIAS'S HEAD was still spinning, and it seemed like it had been for months now.

"Are you about ready to go?" James asked from behind him.

Mattias slowly turned away from the Christmas tree in James's—no, *their*—living room. Mattias had let his apartment go and moved in with James just two weeks ago, and he was still getting used to his new living space… and sleeping with James every night. He actually yawned and covered his mouth with his hand. James had a tendency to keep them both up long after they had gone to bed. Not that Mattias was complaining, not for an instant.

"We're going to be late," James prodded gently. "And the sheriff will forgive a lot of things, but not tardiness, especially to his victory party." He winked and smiled.

"Your boss has been on cloud nine since being elected sheriff, and you know it." After all the revelations about his father, James had thought it best to leave the Mechanicsburg PD. Solly was thrilled to have him, so James had transitioned a month ago. There were no hard feelings on either side, but some of his colleagues didn't understand how James could deal with his father... so it was best to leave. And some distance seemed to have been what was needed.

"Who celebrates an election victory on New Year's Eve?" Mattias teased.

"There hasn't been time since the election, and Solly figured he might as well combine the celebrations. You know him—he's efficient if nothing else." James smiled and slipped his arms around Mattias's waist and under his sweater. "I love having you here. I know it creates a few travel difficulties for you." He nuzzled the base of Mattias's neck, and Mattias knew instantly, not as though there was any doubt, that the benefits far outweighed the troubles.

James stepped away, his arms sliding from around Mattias's waist. "I have something that came today. I meant it as a Christmas present, but I waited too late to order it. It just came." James hurried into the kitchen and returned with a small box. He opened it and handed the contents to Mattias. It was a leather wrist cuff with silver decoration. "A friend lives in Albuquerque, and she arranged to get it for me. It's one of a kind, and I wanted to give you something to say how much I appreciate you standing by me through this whole huge family drama."

Mattias was stunned. The cuff was gorgeous, and he extended his arm so James could put it on him. Then he leaned in and kissed James hard enough that he wondered if they could just skip the party and go upstairs. Of course they couldn't, and James got their warm coats and they left.

The fallout from Elias's arrest had been nuclear. As soon as James's mother found out what had been happening, she refused to help Elias and had apparently emptied their bank accounts and made sure that Elias couldn't use any assets that had her name on them. As a result, and the fact that Elias lived out of state, he was still sitting in jail pending trial, and James's mother had filed for divorce. Thankfully she had decided to stay in Florida. He and James were planning to leave in a few days to spend some winter vacation time with her. James had told him that he had seen his father only twice, and both times had been accidental. James said he had no intention of spending any quality jail time with him.

It had been especially hard on James; Mattias had known that pretty clearly. James had spent years looking the other way, and guilt combined with plenty of recrimination had weighed on him for weeks. Mattias hoped that visiting his mother would help him. What had happened wasn't James's fault.

They left through the back and trudged through fresh snow to the garage. Thankfully it had stopped falling, but the entire world seemed clean and new under its blanket of white. In the garage, they got into James's car, cranked the heat, and drove carefully to the Mayapple Country Club, where the sheriff had reserved a room for the evening. The drive took longer than expected because of the snow on the roads, but they parked and went inside.

"Uncle Mattias!" Justine said as she hurried over with Kim and her brother, Claude, right behind her. Mattias hugged the little girl tightly while Claude went to James. Then they switched once hugs had been dispensed.

"They have been asking for you all evening," Kim said, giving each of them a hug. The change in the two kids they had discovered during the robbery attempt was stunning. Kim's husband, Albert, followed them and shook hands with each of them.

"Miss Kim says that she and Mr. Albert are going to keep us," Justine said, jumping up and down in her excitement.

Kim knelt down. "We've talked about this. Mr. Albert and I are going to be your long-term foster parents until the courts decide what they are going to do." She hugged the little girl, looking up at Mattias from over Justine's shoulder. It was pretty clear that Kim had developed an attachment to the kids that went pretty deep.

"I know. But we don't have to go to another foster home." She stuck out her tongue, and Mattias laughed.

"Miss Kim is good to you, isn't she?" Mattias asked, his heart doing a damned skip around the room at how happy the four of them were. Justine nodded and chose that moment to get shy.

Kim extended her hand, and Justine took it. James and Mattias followed them to a table and sat down. Over the past few months, he and James had become friends with Kim and Albert, along with the kids. If things worked out, she had told them that she and Albert would provide a permanent home for the kids. But that was a long way out at this point. Still, Claude and Justine had a chance at a good life, and that warmed Mattias's heart more than he could possibly say.

James seemed to know his thoughts and took his hand under the table, squeezing it lightly. They shared a moment before returning their attention to the others.

A glass clinked, and Sheriff Solly Briggs stood with a huge smile. "I know it took a while to put everything together, but what better night to celebrate new beginnings and the future than New Year's Eve? I want to thank everyone who made my election possible. It's a dream come true for me, and I'm eternally grateful for the opportunity and the faith you've all shown in me. This next year holds a lot of promise for all of us." The sheriff raised his glass, and everyone in the room joined in as well.

Mattias turned to James, grinned, and lightly clinked his glass, then did the same with Kim, Albert, and each of the kids. Before drinking, he shared a kiss with James. The sheriff had hit the nail on the head. The future did indeed look bright, no matter how Mattias looked at it. He sipped his sparkling wine and rested his head on James's shoulder. Promise indeed.

Keep reading for an excerpt from
Fire and Onyx
by Andrew Grey

CHAPTER 1

EVAN WHITTAKER'S gut churned, hard, and he had to work to suppress it. Weeks of effort, and he could see the whole thing going down the fucking drain right before his eyes. Officers stormed the ramshackle house two miles west of Carlisle, where the suspects had been not two hours before. And the biggest pile of shit of all, Sheriff Briggs had backed him and he'd been wrong—and now it was pretty clear that the house was empty and the suspects had moved on.

Pierre kicked in the front door, and the deputies surged forward; another team led by Clay would be coming through the back. Evan could see it all playing out just as planned, but without the suspects.

"Clear" rang through the house as room after room was checked.

"Where the hell did they go?" Pierre asked when they met in the living room, which had been ripped to hell, with huge holes in the walls and the carpet trashed. "We had eyes on them the whole time."

Evan groaned. Someone had messed up, and he was sure this was going to end up coming down on his shoulders—not that he could blame anyone. The sheriff had gone out on a limb, and Evan could hear it snapping out from under him.

"Ravelle, Whitaker, you better come down here," one of the deputies called. "Be careful, though."

Evan made his way to the basement stairs, which were rickety beyond belief. He went down, shivering in the dusty, rustic space. "Damn it all…." Part of the foundation had been removed and shored up to leave a tunnel of sorts. Evan was willing to bet that they'd gotten out there and disappeared into the surrounding wooded area. It would have taken maybe a few minutes and they would be out.

"Check out in the woods," Pierre ordered, but Evan was pretty sure their suspects were long gone. All that they were left with was a house that had been used to cook meth and little else. At least he hadn't been wrong about what the house was being used for. That might keep his ass in one piece, but it was definitely going to get chewed on. He should have thought of an escape route and looked for it.

"Shit," one of the men called from above as smoke billowed through the door. The deputies went up the steps, and they crashed back through to the dirt floor.

"Are both of you okay?" Evan asked, helping Phillips, the deputy nearest to him, to his feet. He brushed himself off, and Evan pointed him toward the tunnel. "Get the hell out of here. This place is going to be an inferno." Already the roar of flames sounded overhead, and Evan hoped to hell everyone else got out, because this house was going to burn down around them otherwise. "You too." He helped Pierre get Phillips out. He was covered in dirt and walking gingerly. "I'll be right behind."

Phillips went through the hole, and Evan pointed for Pierre to go next as embers and burning debris fell through the hole that had been the stairs. Already the air was fouling, the roar increasing from above. Evan bent and crawled along the dirt passage, and emerged to clouds of smoke whirling around them on the breeze. The others were already helping Phillips away from the conflagration, and the officers made their way around the edge of the property to where the rest of the responding team had gathered in front.

"Is everyone out?" Evan asked, joining the other men as the old house nearly self-destructed. Before the fire department could arrive, the place was fully engulfed and the roof was already caving in. Just another craptastic thing to add to the list of the screwups of the day.

"Yes," Pierre told him. "We aren't getting anything from that scene, but everyone is safe."

At least that was something. Too bad Phillips was injured.

"An ambulance is on the way," Pierre relayed, and then acknowledged a radio confirmation.

"What the hell happened?" Evan asked, turning to the other deputies.

"Checking the last room in the back, I pulled open the closet, and it was rigged with lighter fluid," Clay explained.

Evan nodded. There wasn't a damned thing they could have done. This had clearly been planned, and they had fallen into it. "I want these sons of bitches so bad, I can taste it." He clamped his jaws together in frustration.

"At least no one else will be using this place as a hideout."

The fire department arrived, and the outer walls collapsed as they began spraying water. Evan dreaded the report he was going to have to write. A big, fat nothing. That was what they had, after weeks of work and all this effort—a pile of ash and no suspects.

A call came through the radio. "The suspects appear to have had cars waiting and are long gone."

The nail in the coffin of this fucked-up day, and to make matters worse, the sky opened up, dumping a torrent of rain all over everything and everyone. Evan ran to the car, pulled on his rain gear, and waited while the fire department doused the remaining fire, which died quickly. Once he had secured the scene, he drove back to the station. It didn't help his foul mood that the sheriff was waiting for him and he received the chewing out he expected.

"I'm not angry that the bust broke down, but you should have been more prepared and checked for an escape route. It's pretty classic," Briggs said when he calmed down. "Now we've got nothing at all. Most of the evidence burned in the fire, so we have little to track them with, and anything they left behind—"

"Sheriff," Evan interrupted, "there is one thing they definitely left behind: the business itself. There's no way they're going to just walk away. They packed up shop in that location, but they're still going to need to fill the demand they created, or someone else will step in." At least he could track them through their product.

Sheriff Briggs leaned forward. "We've been dealing with these assholes for two years now, and every time we get close, they scamper away and crawl back under some rock, only to surface again. I want them stopped—*now*. So you figure out how in the hell we're going to do that. People are scared, especially folks out in the county where they operate, and if we don't put an end to this, then the people of this county are going to put an end to me."

The truth was that Briggs had fought and worked hard for his job, and he deserved it, as far as Evan was concerned. The difficult part about this whole damned thing was disappointing the sheriff. The entire department respected him greatly. He wasn't just elected, but had been part of the department and knew the county like the back of his hand.

"And I thought we had them."

"Which is when things usually fall apart." Sheriff Briggs placed his hands on his desk. "Go back to the drawing board, and come up with a way to put an end to these guys." His gaze bored into Evan. "This can't be allowed to continue in this area. Whoever is behind this shit is making fools of us. They seem to know where we're going to strike and are always one step ahead of us."

"Yes. I know we had a leak that we plugged a while ago, but…." Evan was well aware that guys like these had plenty of money and were willing to spread it around to buy support and protection. It was also possible that they were using leverage of some sort against a cop or their family in order to gain cooperation. "I'll go through everything again, and if there is someone working with these people, I'll find them." He set his jaw, knowing the look he was giving the sheriff. Turncoats absolutely made his blood boil. Evan believed in the brotherhood of officers, and someone like that put them all at risk.

"I'll be doing the same. But as far as I can tell, it's possible that they have deduced our movements and that we're dealing with someone really smart who knows the area." Sheriff Briggs leaned back in his chair.

"I agree." The wheels were already turning. "Maybe we can put those two things together and come up with someone who might fit the bill. If they knew the area, especially between Carlisle and Newville…." An idea was forming, but Evan didn't have quite enough information. He couldn't track down every smart person in the damned county.

"I'd concentrate on people out near Newville and the surrounding area. See if anyone has seen anything or if they've noticed any suspicious activity. Talk to a few community leaders. It's a small community, and people definitely talk. Someone out there knows who this guy is and is sheltering him right now. You know that, and so do I. There's no way he can exist in the community unless that's happening."

"I'm on it." Evan figured he was getting off lucky. Though this wasn't directly his fault, it was his investigation, so he was responsible for the results—good and bad.

"Write your report and get it filed. Then go home and get some rest. Be here fresh in the morning, ready to take a new look at this." Briggs turned to his computer, and Evan left his office.

"How bad was it?" Pierre asked as soon as he closed the door.

Evan shrugged. "The thing I can't stand is letting Briggs down after he went to bat for me." He'd had no way of knowing about the escape in the basement. The exit aboveground was surrounded by thick bushes, and it wasn't likely to have been visible even from a drone. It happened, and they all needed to learn from it. "At least I'll know what to look for next time."

"That's true." Pierre turned, heading toward his desk, then paused. "Jordan asked me to remind you that we were supposed to have dinner tonight with his friend Marcus."

Evan groaned. Everyone from his friends to his mother had decided to fix him up in the last three months. "I know I agreed, but another one?"

"Since your breakup with Antonio... well, you're on the market and a catch." Pierre grinned. Apparently any gay deputy who wasn't currently in a relationship was a catch. Or maybe it was some sort of huge betting pool to see who could get Evan his next boyfriend. He wasn't sure what the prize could be, though.

"Peachy," he muttered. "Where are we meeting?"

"Café Belgie at six thirty." Pierre walked back toward him. "And after this, I promise I'll tell Jordan that this is the end. No more fixups. I had asked him not to do this, but you know Jordan when he sets his mind to something. He thinks you and Marcus will be perfect together. Though he said the same thing about Brad, and look how that turned out." Pierre actually snickered, the bastard.

Brad was indeed a nice guy, at least in public, but in private he was bossy, egotistical, and thought that he was God's gift to men in general and that they should all bow down before him... in more ways than one.

Needless to say, he and Brad had had no additional dates.

"Yeah, thanks for that. If it's that bad...." He trailed off into a growl.

"Don't worry. Marcus is a nice guy." Pierre hurried away, and Evan had plenty of time to wonder just what he might have meant by that. Was everything in his life turning into complete and total crap? He really hoped not, but things weren't looking good.

EVAN HAD showered and changed clothes, then walked the three blocks to Café Belgie and went inside. "Hey, Billy."

"Another fixup?" Billy asked.

"Yeah. Jordan is determined. Pierre says this is the last one, so maybe I'll get lucky." Evan wasn't holding his breath.

When Billy motioned to the table back in the corner, he groaned as Marcus stood up. Their eyes met, and Marcus smiled and then laughed. Apparently neither of them had made the connection.

Evan approached the table. "Jordan, I take it you didn't show Marcus here a picture."

"No, why?"

"Because if you had, I could have told you that Evan and I dated for exactly a week about two months ago." Marcus sat back down, and Evan took the seat that was designated for him. "Evan is a nice guy, but he and I… there isn't that spark." Thankfully, Marcus was as amused about this as he was, and Evan figured he could have a decent evening with friends and then go home.

"That's enough fixups, Jordan," Pierre said. "Evan knows that we love him."

"Yeah, and he needs to find someone who will…." Jordan sighed. "I just want him to be as happy as I am."

Sometimes Jordan was just adorable, and the way he gazed at Pierre, as though he were the center of the world, was nearly overwhelming. Yes, Evan wanted to find someone, but his luck with guys was so abysmal that he had pretty much given up. He had read somewhere that unhappiness was the difference between what you had and what you expected, and since he no longer expected to meet someone, he couldn't classify himself as unhappy. Too bad everyone else seemed to.

"Where is Jeremiah tonight?" Evan asked, trying to change the subject. There was nothing he could do about this evening except make the best of it.

"He's with the sitter. Before Megan got there, he was upset because we were leaving, but as soon as she arrived, that came to an end. They were playing games when we left, and he barely noticed us going."

Pierre chuckled. "I think he likes her."

Jordan shivered. "I don't even want to think about that right now. He's too young to be interested in girls already." It was pretty clear that Jordan wasn't ready for his son to enter that stage of life. Still, it was cute to see him a little flustered. Jordan was an amazing parent, and so was Pierre, for that matter.

"What have you been doing with yourself?" Marcus asked.

"Working a lot." Evan so didn't want to go into the mess that happened today. That was just something he wasn't prepared for. He needed this to be a good evening, and thankfully Pierre seemed to have the same idea and mentioned nothing about it.

THE DINNER had been pleasant, but Evan was really happy to be home, where he could put his feet up and not have to worry about being on for someone else.

His phone rang as soon as he closed the front door, and Evan continued through his row house living room, dining room, and kitchen to the back sitting room, answering the phone as he flopped into his comfy chair. "Hey, Mom, isn't it a little late?"

"It's eleven, and I'm not so in my dotage that I don't stay up to watch *Conan*. I like him. If I were younger, I'd probably take him for a test drive, maybe kick his tires a little." She cackled, knowing that hearing her talk about men was a little discomforting for him. Evan had decided to ignore it, figuring it was just for effect. "I saw that you just got home." His mother lived next door, and Evan figured her hobby was watching his comings and goings.

"Don't you have anything better to do than watch for me?" he challenged.

"Oh, get over yourself. I just got home too. I was out with Hector. We went dancing at the VFW. They had a swing band, and that man has rhythm."

Evan refused to think of just the kind of rhythm his mother was referring to.

"Were you out on a date?"

"Were you?" he retorted.

"Don't be cheeky." The delight in her voice told him that he'd hit the mark.

"When do I get to meet him so I can determine his intentions? I know the two of you have been out a couple of times, so you must enjoy his company." Evan wasn't letting just anyone date his mother.

"His intentions. Please…. First thing, I will decide what his intentions are, and secondly, he and I just went dancing. That's all there is to it. You do not get to scare him off with all of that talk about being a cop… and don't you dare run a background check on him."

He had done that a few times.

"How am I supposed to know if he's good enough for my mama if you don't let me meet him and I can't check him out? What if he's some sort of serial killer?" He had to tease; it was too much fun. "Okay, Mom, no background checks—on one condition. No more fixups from you."

He got silence in return.

"Okay," she finally agreed. "But how am I supposed to get grandchildren? Your taste in men… well, it sucks and you know it. Sometimes I swear you're a loser magnet. Look at the guys you've brought home and tell me I'm wrong." She paused for dramatic effect, and Evan wished he could argue with her. The men he'd dated all started out nice and then morphed into the spawn of Satan. "So I asked your nice friends for help."

"Yeah, and one of them fixed me up with a guy that I was already fixed up with," he groused. "And how does me finding a guy get you grandchildren? You know there is no uterus involved, right?"

"Smartass. There are plenty of children that need good homes, and I will be a spectacular grandmother and you know it. Forget that milk-and-cookies crap— I'll get a sidecar for the Harley and hit the road."

Evan stifled a groan because there wasn't a damned thing he could do about the truth. His mother had discovered the joy of motorcycles after his father passed away five years ago, and had turned into a Harley Mama overnight. He swore the only reason she wore a helmet was to keep the road dirt out of her hair.

"Just back off, okay? This pressure is getting too much." His head throbbed slightly, and he closed his eyes for a second.

"There's no pressure." She sounded sweet as candy, but Evan knew it was a lie.

"Yes, there is, and you know it. I…. Just back off and let me have a chance to breathe. Things are rough at work right now…."

"Yeah, I heard at the VFW. The guy slipped through your fingers." She snorted. "This asshole is a slick devil, but you'll get him in the end, I know it. And I'll keep my eyes open. There might be talk."

"Mom…."

"You don't think I know what some of the guys in the club are into? They love me and tell me shit that would curl your hair if you had any." She laughed again, and Evan wondered how much his mother had had to drink.

"That's not a bad idea," he said softly. "Do you see that kind of thing in the club? I'm not asking you to rat on anyone, but I need an in with this group and I'll take anything right now. These people are bad news, like a lot of folks are getting hurt… bad."

"You want me to try to score something? I can and see what it gets me."

There were times when his mother shocked the living hell out of him, and this was one of them. "No. Do nothing illegal, whatever you do. Just listen and let me know if you hear anything. Maybe talk to a few friends, see if they know anything." His mother was the queen of wheedling secrets out of people. She was five foot with a great smile, and she could charm the bees out of their honey. "I'm probably going to try undercover if I can figure out a way in."

"You know I'll help." She yawned through the line, which was contagious. "I'll talk to you later. I'm going to get my butt in bed so I can be raring to go tomorrow. I'm going for a ride north over the mountains. Up is fun, but down is a thrill and a half." She ended the call, and Evan set his phone on the coffee table, wondering just how he was going to infiltrate an organization he couldn't seem to get a finger on, let alone find an opening he could exploit. What he needed was info, and he knew someone who might be able to provide it… for a price.

ANDREW GREY is the author of more than 100 works of Contemporary Gay Romantic fiction. After twenty-seven years in corporate America, he has now settled down in Central Pennsylvania with his husband, Dominic, and his laptop. An interesting ménage. Andrew grew up in western Michigan with a father who loved to tell stories and a mother who loved to read them. Since then he has lived throughout the country and traveled throughout the world. He is a recipient of the RWA Centennial Award, has a master's degree from the University of Wisconsin-Milwaukee, and now writes full-time. Andrew's hobbies include collecting antiques, gardening, and leaving his dirty dishes anywhere but in the sink (particularly when writing). He considers himself blessed with an accepting family, fantastic friends, and the world's most supportive and loving partner. Andrew currently lives in beautiful, historic Carlisle, Pennsylvania.

Email: andrewgrey@comcast.net
Website: www.andrewgreybooks.com

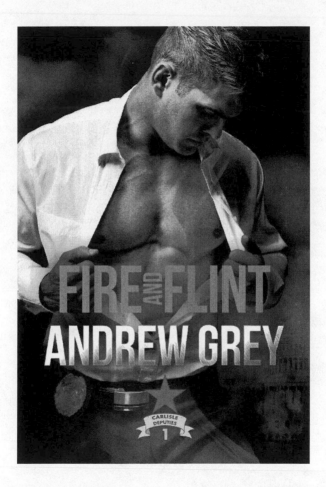

A Carlisle Deputies Novel

Jordan Erichsohn suspects something is rotten about his boss, Judge Crawford. Unfortunately he has nowhere to turn and doubts anyone will believe his claims—least of all the handsome deputy, Pierre Ravelle, who has been assigned to protect the judge after he received threatening letters. The judge has a long reach, and if he finds out Jordan's turned on him, he might impede Jordan adopting his son, Jeremiah.

When Jordan can no longer stay silent, he gathers his courage and tells Pierre what he knows. To his surprise and relief, Pierre believes him, and Jordan finds an ally… and maybe more. Pierre vows to do what it takes to protect Jordan and Jeremiah and see justice done. He's willing to fight for the man he's growing to love and the family he's starting to think of as his own. But Crawford is a powerful and dangerous enemy, and he's not above ripping apart everything Jordan and Pierre are trying to build in order to save himself….

www.dreamspinnerpress.com

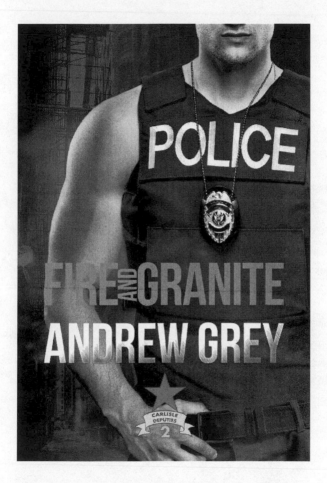

A Carlisle Deputies Novel

The heat is growing from the inside, but danger is building on the outside.

Judge Andrew Phillips runs a tight ship in his courtroom. He's tough, and when he hands down a sentence, he expects to be obeyed. So when a fugitive named Harper escapes and threatens his life, Andrew isn't keen on twenty-four/seven protection… especially not from Deputy Clay Brown. They have a past, one that could cause problems in their careers.

But with Clay assigned to Andrew and the two of them together every minute, there's nowhere to hide from their attraction—or from the fact that there's much more than chemistry blooming between them. As the threat intensifies, Clay knows he'll do anything it takes to protect the people who are taking their places in his heart: Andrew and his young niece and nephew.

www.dreamspinnerpress.com

A Carlisle Deputies Novel

When Chris Anducci is moved off jail duty and into the sheriff's office, he doesn't expect his first assignment to be protecting a witness against a human trafficking ring. Knowing the new sheriff doesn't abide screwups, Chris reluctantly agrees to work the case.

Pavle Kasun has spent the last four years of his life at the mercy of others. When an opportunity presented itself, he took it, resulting in his rescue. Now the safe houses he's placed in are being threatened and he needs protection if he is to have any sort of chance at a life.

Chris opens his home to Pavle, but he doesn't expect Pavle and his story to get under his skin… and stay there. Soon they discover they have more in common than either of them thought. Slowly Pavle comes out of his shell and Chris finds someone who touches his heart. But as the men looking for Pavle close in, they will stop at nothing to get him out of the way. But even if Chris can keep him safe, he might not be able to protect his heart if Pavle moves back home.

www.dreamspinnerpress.com

A Carlisle Deputies Novel

When Deputy Nick Senaster chastises a bunch of college kids at a bar, he doesn't think anything of it, even if their leader is gorgeous. The guy is too young and way too cocky, and soon Nick has an emergency foster placement to focus on. His first job is ensuring ten-year-old Ethan knows someone cares for him. But Nick doesn't realize Ethan is a package deal.

When Alexander finds out his abusive stepfather, Dieter, has lost custody of his half brother, he's torn between relief and dread. Alexander can't get custody until he can provide a home for his tiny family. In the meantime, at least Ethan's foster father will let Alexander visit.

So of course the man turns out to be the cute but dour cop who gave Alexander a hard time.

Soon Nick and Alexander discover they misjudged each other. Nick is more than an authoritarian automaton, and Alexander has a drive and a maturity that belie their first meeting. But between a campaign of intimidation from Dieter, their own insecurities, and the logistics of dating with Ethan's fragile sense of stability hanging in the balance, they have their work cut out for them if they want to build a future.

www.dreamspinnerpress.com